Fears and Phantoms

Eleanor Jones

Fears and Phantoms

ISBN: 1-933343-20-6

Stabenfeldt, Inc.
457 North Main Street
Danbury, CT 06811
www.pony.us

chapter one

Tilly's long slim fingers curled around the twisted bar, gripping the cold hard ridges of metal as she gave the wrought iron gate a violent push. It swung shut with a satisfying clang and she closed her eyes tightly as the echoing sound rang around inside her head, penetrating the dull fog of misery that clouded her brain.

She wanted to shout. She wanted to scream. She wanted to yell out her anger. How could her mother have done that to her? How could she have turned her whole life upside down without a second thought?

While the world shuddered slowly back into silence again, broken only by the rush of a breeze through the treetops above her head, Tilly remained totally still, a waiflike, vulnerable figure, against the imposing ornate structure of the gate. There was no point in shouting out into the empty silence that surrounded her, for who was there to listen? Stifling a sob she turned to press her face into the warm salty wetness of Sunny's neck. Somehow she had to deal with this, and deal with it alone... for there was no one else who cared.

The big dun gelding stood steaming in the autumn sunshine. His golden coat was darkly streaked with sweat and his strange, amber colored eyes flickered restlessly as he waited for his mistress to spring into the saddle. They always cantered along the pathway through the woods, his iron shod hooves thudding softly on the carpet of leaves as he strained against the bridle. Now he nudged Tilly roughly, pushing her hard against the bars of the gate in his impatience to be off.

"Hey!"

She eased her bruised shoulder with the palm of her hand, meeting his inquisitive gaze with a frown of annoyance. He sidled in response, pulling back hard on the reins, and a sense of wild recklessness pierced her despair.

"You want a gallop, boy…?"

Her deep blue eyes darkened almost to purple and she reached for the stirrup. Suddenly she desperately needed to feel the surge of power beneath her as Sunny's muscles bulged with effort. Needed to hear the thunder of his hooves in her ears. Needed to race away from the misery that overwhelmed her.

Infected by her crazy mood, the big gelding plunged as she swung into the saddle. She wrapped her legs around his heaving ribcage, urging him forward, and his powerful quarters bunched beneath him.

"Come on, then…!"

Her defiant cry rose to the treetops, challenging life itself, echoing deep into the very heart of the woodland where it touched a chord in a kindred spirit. And as the dun gelding's metal shod hooves thudded across the carpet of gold and brown, a dark-eyed girl gave an inward sigh and turned her face toward the distant sound.

Unaware that someone had heard her cry – unaware, in fact, of anything but a desperate need to try to escape from the black cloud that consumed her – Tilly crouched low over Sunny's withers. She breathed in his warm, horsy aroma, ignoring the stinging lash of the long brown mane that whipped against her face.

The pounding of hooves thundered in her ears, shuddering throughout her whole body, and she reveled in the sound.

Moving with the rhythm. Eyes half closed. Wanting nothing more than to be totally one with the horse beneath her as he stretched out along the pathway through the center of Crickle Wood. Then, suddenly, the path was gone and they were struggling through dense undergrowth. Brushing past trees. Stumbling on uneven ground. Her eyes flew wide open. She tried to get her bearings. What was happening…? Where were they?

Sunny's whole body tensed beneath her. He floundered on, lost and confused. When and how had they left the pathway…?

A fierce crackling sound was loud in their ears, almost upon them, but there was nothing to see. Sunny leaped to the side. Tilly lurched down his neck, grabbing his mane as she went. Struggling to regain her balance. Hauling on the reins as she tried to turn him back the way they had come. All she could see around her was dense foliage; blackberry bushes heavy with overripe fruit, saplings huddled closely together amidst ancient tree trunks that leaned dangerously over, blocking their route. How had she come to this place? How had they strayed so easily from the broad, familiar pathway?

Way overhead a bird trilled in a high-pitched tone. She took a deep breath, leaning down to run her hand along the taut line of Sunny's crest.

"Don't worry, boy," she told him, glancing uneasily at the unfamiliar surroundings. The birdsong ceased abruptly and a deep impenetrable silence settled heavily, forcing the breath from her lungs.

"Come on," she urged.

The horse beneath her snorted loudly before stepping un-willingly forward; eyes on stalks and tail raised behind him like a banner. Her legs tightened around his heaving rib cage. She gathered up the reins, and as the acrid smell of smoke curled up her nostrils she heard the crackling sound again, only now it seemed to be all around them.

"Come on," she cried again.

Her heart beat a tattoo inside her chest as Sunny obliged; leaping forward into the flurry of sparks that showered over them like golden rain. Fire was everywhere. Curling through the trees. Licking the branches with tongues of flame. Scorching the undergrowth beneath their feet. Tilly just leaned down low over Sunny's neck and kicked him forward.

"Come on, boy," she screamed. "You can do it!"

No time to think. No time to plan. Carried along on a wave of desperation to survive, Sunny leaped into a crazy gallop while Tilly clung helplessly to the long tendrils of his flying mane.

Faster and faster they went. Stumbling over rocks and the mossy, overgrown stumps of trees long dead. Leaping over fallen trunks that barred their way.

At last the crackling sounds died away behind them, and slivers of light, replacing the clinging gray smoke fumes, filtered through the tree-top canopy high overhead,

As the horror of fire receded, Tilly's heartbeat slowed just a little. Sunny's pounding hooves hit the familiar pathway, and she sat up in the saddle with a flood of relief, easing back on the reins. At last they were safe. But the big dun gelding had other ideas. He was way beyond reason. Head raised in panic and ears flattened against his skull, he leaped into a gallop, all other senses eclipsed by the flight instinct that drove him.

Tilly hauled on the reins. Trying to keep a clear head. Pulling and releasing and pulling again until her hands were bruised and sore. Screaming at him to him to "whoa!" But as the pathway widened he just lengthened his stride and they hurtled on toward the metal gate.

Just ahead now she could hear the busy hum of traffic on the main road – thank goodness for the gate! But would he be able to stop in time? An image of them crashing into the metal bars filled her mind, and she doubled her efforts to slow down.

The powerful horse could have been made of wood for all the notice he took as they thundered around the final corner... Then suddenly, to her horror, she saw just ahead of them an open gap! The gate was gone. The Millennium gate had disappeared and there was no barrier between the galloping horse and the roar of traffic that flashed by only yards away from them now.

A kind of helplessness rushed through Tilly's veins. She clung to the terrified creature beneath her and a roaring sound filled her ears. The scream of brakes and tires sliding on pavement flooded her imagination... the image of Sunny, broken and bleeding, or worse. She stood in the stirrups, screaming at him to stop before it was too late. Yanking desperately on the reins. And then she saw her! A small figure in the center of the pathway just ahead, motionless against the flash of moving traffic.

"Look out!" Tilly cried.

Her voice echoed through the treetops but the girl remained totally still, head flung back and feet planted slightly apart as if rooted into the carpet of leaves upon which she stood. Like a tree, thought Tilly ridiculously. This girl was staring, mesmerized. Couldn't she see the danger she was in?

As the distance between them decreased the girl appeared to grow in stature, raising her arms and staring, totally unafraid, at the horse that careered toward her. To Tilly, time seemed suddenly suspended in dawning horror. Would they still gallop out into the traffic after they had mown the girl down, or would trampling on a human being bring Sunny suddenly to his senses? She had to try and do something.

"Get out of the way...!"

Her voice was a distant scream in her ears.

"Get out of the way," she yelled again, but the girl just seemed to root herself more firmly. Raising her arms ever higher, totally silent and so sure of her actions.

Maybe it was that very confidence that did it, or maybe it was some deeper force, but something certainly penetrated the frozen panic that had totally taken Sunny over. Just in the moment when it seemed that the girl would surely be trampled beneath his flying hooves, he dug in his toes, sliding toward her, rearing up above the motionless figure that stared up at him, undaunted. All Tilly could see as she threw her weight forward and clung like a leech was the pale face below them, and dark eyes, blazing into hers with fierce determination. Was that what had saved their lives, that sheer intensity of spirit?

Sunny seemed then suddenly to shrink beneath her. His flailing hooves thudded back onto the thick carpet of damp leaves. The dark-haired girl reached out for his rein, making a soft clucking sound and he lowered his head, breathing heavily, while Tilly slid to the ground on legs of jelly that crumpled beneath her.

"You OK?"

At the note of soft concern in the girl's voice Tilly felt tears well up behind her eyes. She stared hard at the ground, her teeth digging unheeded into her bottom lip, and when a comforting hand reached out to touch her shoulder a great wracking sob shuddered through her slight frame.

"Don't feel bad," insisted the girl in a gentle tone. "You could have been killed. Anyone would be a bit upset."

"But the gate… where's the gate?"

"Gate…?" The girl looked vacantly in the direction of the road. "What gate?"

Tilly felt a rush of impatience.

"The Millennium gate."

Sunny lowered his head to nibble at the tufts of grass beside the path, as if the trauma of the last few minutes (was it merely minutes?) had never even happened. A comforting cloak of normality settled around her.

11

The girl stood quite still, real enough, her legs still firmly planted a foot apart and her round face turned determinedly in the direction of the road, cheeks pink against the paleness of her skin.

"They *should* put a gate there," she declared with a firm nod. "That road is so busy nowadays."

"But there is…" Tilly's shoulders drooped. "It was made especially for the new millennium. It must be on a different pathway or something… There was a fire, you see."

"Fire…?"

The girl tugged at Sunny's rein, dragging his head up from the grass.

"Come on," she insisted. "You've had a shock. Let's go where it's a bit safer and you can tell me what is really wrong."

How did she know that something was wrong? Tilly glanced across and met understanding in her soft, dark eyes.

"Horses don't bolt for nothing. Something bad must have happened to trigger it."

"It was the fire…" started Tilly and then she remembered how, even before the fire, the pathway had simply seemed to disappear. "At least…"

The girl took firmly hold of her arm.

"Just take a few deep breaths and try not to think about it," she suggested. You're safe now – that's all that really matters."

Tilly struggled to her feet, embarrassed by the strange weakness in her legs and ashamed of the weepy feeling that kept on coming over her in waves. Sunny seemed totally calm as the girl led the way through the trees. He wandered along behind them, grabbing for grass, as if this were another ordinary day and they hadn't both just been through the worst experience of their entire lives.

They left the main pathway behind them and turned onto another narrow track where the trees hung low above their heads. The hum of traffic faded. The silence of the woodland settled around them again, and Tilly felt herself begin to relax, just a little. Her eyes fell upon the stalwart figure that marched ahead, and a flood of gratitude brought the weepy feeling back again.

"What is your name?" she called, suddenly needing to know more about the girl who had acted so bravely and saved both their lives.

"Bess," was the brief response. "My name's Bess."

"And I'm Matilda… Matilda McCloud. But everyone calls me Tilly."

The girl stopped and looked at her directly, her round, pleasant face framed by a tousled mop of dark, glossy curls above and a bright, canary yellow polo necked shirt below. She wore loose fitting beige jodhpurs and short brown boots; old fashioned looking, decided Tilly, and somehow very dependable.

"Well, *Matilda* McCloud," she announced with a warm smile. "Why don't we sit down on that log over there and you can tell me exactly what is wrong."

What was wrong? Tilly's chin slumped onto her chest. What was right was more like it.

chapter two

The two girls sat in silence, side by side on the ivy-covered, rotting log, while Sunny grazed contentedly beside them, his reins firmly held by Bess. Tilly felt strangely distanced at first, numb with shock, but as the reality of their close escape slowly dawned, the numbness was replaced by an acute awareness.

Bark, rough beneath her fingers. Vapor, rising in clouds from the steaming horse, wafting into the clear, crisp air. The aroma of wood, damp from a shower of rain, and autumn fruits, bursting with ripeness – real living things that would have meant nothing without Sunny.

Made bold by the stillness of the two humans on the log and unperturbed by the grazing horse, a squirrel dashed along a nearby branch. Tilly focused on it, trying to close her heart to the misery that hovered. Trying to forget that her whole life was falling apart.

Bess was not so easily deceived. "Well?" she announced brightly. "Come on, a problem shared is a problem solved, so they say." Tilly looked down at her hands, twisting them nervously together, fumbling deep inside her brain for the right words.

"We used to be happy," she eventually began. "Mom and Dad and me… and Sunny."

"That's a good name for him," interrupted Bess.

They turned as one toward the golden dun gelding who looked now as if butter wouldn't melt in his mouth.

"We bought him when he was just three years old," continued Tilly with growing confidence. "He was so wild. My Mom was furious when Dad and I brought him home from the sale."

A brief smile flitted across her face as she remembered the gawky golden colt with frightened eyes.

"And you broke him in yourself?"

Tilly nodded "I thought I knew him so well… until today."

"Horses are like that, though, aren't they?" remarked Bess. "Always wild, deep down."

Tilly stared at Sunny, searching his face for a sign of *his* wildness. It had been so apparent just a short time ago. He looked back at her with wide, trusting eyes, and she nodded.

"Yes," she agreed doubtfully. "Yes… at least… I suppose they must be."

"So what went wrong?" prompted Bess.

Tilly's twisting fingers locked together, and she transferred her gaze toward them, teeth clenched tight shut.

"My dad lost his job in the city," she eventually blurted out. "That's why we moved here, to Burnbrook village. We didn't have as much money as before, but Millside, our house, is really nice. And the stable board is cheaper, so it did mean that I could still have a horse…"

"Even though it *is* one that bolts with you," cut in Bess with a smile.

Tilly glanced up, her eyes dark with emotion, and then they lightened just a little.

"Even though it is one that bolts with me," she agreed with the ghost of a smile.

"So what went wrong?" repeated Bess.

She sucked in a deep breath of air.

"My parents are splitting up!"

There, she had said it. She had finally shared the secret that was eating her heart out. Misery clawed at her. "And my mother says we have to sell Sunny."

"But of course you aren't going to!"

Bess's firmly spoken words took Tilly by surprise. She had expected sympathy.

"We… we just can't afford him anymore, and my mother… My mother doesn't understand, she's just so…"

"Angry and confused?" cut in Bess.

Tilly hadn't thought of it like that. Was her mother angry and confused? She felt a rush of guilt at her own selfishness.

"All I've been able to think of is losing Sunny," she admitted.

"So…" Bess thrust out her chin. "You'll just have to fight for him. Your mother probably doesn't know what to do any more than you, but there's always a way. No one can *make* you sell your horse if you don't want to."

"But I have nowhere to keep him," she cried. "That's what she told me today. She can't afford to make next month's stable payment, and neither can my dad."

A sob broke through her defenses and she gulped air.

"She's asked Mr. Cuthbert from the stables to sell him for us," she eventually blurted out, trying to contain the flood that pressed against the back of her whole face.

"Well, if you can't afford the stable then you'll just have to find somewhere cheaper to keep him."

Bess sounded so confident that Tilly felt the tiniest prickle of hope pierce her despair.

"But how… and where?"

Bess shrugged, drawing her thick dark eyebrows together and running her hand across her mouth.

"I don't know… a farm perhaps. There must be farmers around here with fields to spare for one little horse."

A smile flickered across Tilly's face. "Trouble is," she remarked. "He's not so little."

"Or so easy, I suppose," added Bess. "Now if he'd been more like my Domino…"

Guilt prickled again as Tilly realized that she hadn't asked her newfound friend anything about herself.

"You have a horse?" she exclaimed eagerly.

A softness came into Bess's dark eyes and she smiled.

"Yes, and he's the cutest, handsomest, most lovable horse you ever met.

"And…" urged Tilly.

"And he's black and white and very chunky with feathers that grow over his whole hooves and a stripy mane that covers his shoulders."

"So basically nothing like Sunny, then?"

Bess looked up at the fine boned, muscular dun gelding. He raised his lovely head, staring at her with fathomless amber eyes and she shook her head full of glossy curls.

"No… nothing like Sunny. Domino is laid back and on the lazy side, and I know he'll never win me any prizes, but…" She shrugged. "I love him to bits."

"Where is he?" asked Tilly. "Can I see him?"

Bess jumped up eagerly, brushing moss from the seat of her jodhpurs as she tugged Sunny's head up from the grass.

"When I heard you shout I had to take a short cut," she explained. "It was too overgrown to take Dom, so I tied him to a tree. Come on, he's just around the corner."

She walked quickly on ahead and Sunny followed. Hanging back, he wandered lethargically now as if totally deflated by his terrifying experience.

"I wish he was always this quiet," remarked Tilly. Bess glanced back, laughing.

"Well, at least you know how to tire him out now. Get him to bolt through the woods toward a busy main road."

Tilly shivered, wrapping her arms around herself, and glancing up to where the wind moaned softly through the branches way above their heads… an eerie, lonely sound.

"I think I'd rather have him lively," she replied.

18

Sunny's broad golden rump filled the narrow pathway ahead of her. Swaying from side to side, he marched through the dense woodland behind his small, stalwart leader with total confidence.

"Did I thank you for saving us?" she called with a sudden rush of emotion.

"No need to," was the immediate response. "I'm sure you'd have done the same for me."

"Would I?" murmured Tilly, remembering the way the other girl had stood her ground in front of the bolting horse. "I don't think I would have been brave enough."

"You'd be surprised what you can do when you have to," remarked Bess.

The pathway widened. She waited impatiently for Tilly to catch up, as Sunny yanked his head down to sample the short grass that grew on the edge.

"Just as you'll be surprised at what you're able to do to *keep* him," she finished.

A flood of emotion prickled the back of Tilly's eyes. She reached out to run her hand over her precious horse's glorious coat, sticky now with drying sweat, breathing in his aroma as if it was the sweetest nectar in the universe.

"I'll do anything…" Her voice was just a murmur, but it trembled with passion. "Anything at all."

When the branches rustled just beyond them and a low nicker rumbled across the clearing, Sunny's head snapped up from the grass. Ears sharply pricked, he responded with a high-pitched whinny, hauling Bess across to where a stocky piebald cob was tied.

"Here he is," she announced with pride.

The attractive looking gelding turned honest brown eyes toward his mistress, and she handed Sunny's reins over before running across to wrap her arms around Domino's thick neck.

19

"Why!" exclaimed Tilly. "He's exactly as you described him. Right down to the long, stripy mane."

"I told you he was handsome," remarked Bess. Her dark eyes shone and a dull flush colored her pale skin. "I don't know what I'd do if my dad said he had to be sold."

A shadow flitted across Tilly's bright features and she thrust her chin forward.

"You're right," she announced. "Sunny is mine, and no one can force me to sell him."

"That's more like it," cried Bess. "You can't just give in. Put up a fight."

Tilly attempted a smile.

"Can *you* think of a way I can earn some money, or of somewhere else where I could keep him?"

Leaves fluttered down, like silver rain, from the birch tree where the black and white cob was tied, landing softly on Bess's dark hair. She put her head to one side and pursed her lips, one arm draped possessively over his huge neck as he nuzzled her pocket for a piece of the carrot that he knew was in there.

"Cricklewood Farm!" she suddenly announced, withdrawing a large orange chunk and holding it toward him, palm outstretched. "You know… the chicken farm just down the road. They are always looking for people there."

Domino crunched happily.

"What… you mean… to work?" responded Tilly.

Bess laughed out loud. "Of course to work. What did you think I meant? You know the sort of thing. Collecting eggs. Washing eggs. Feeding chickens… *cleaning them out*!"

Tilly nodded vigorously, excitement bubbling inside her.

"All right," she exclaimed. "I get it. And you don't need to look at me like that. I'll do *anything* to keep Sunny. Just point me in the right direction."

"We'll ride to the edge of the woods and I'll show you where it is," offered Bess. "Then I'll have to go, or my father

20

will be wondering where I am, especially if there really *has* been a fire in the woods."

Sensing the uncertainty in her tone Tilly glanced around urgently. Of *course* there had been a fire. But where were the signs now? Her fingers clenched into tight fists, and for a fleeting moment doubt prickled. How had it died away so quickly, and where was the smoke and the scent of charred and burning wood? Shouldn't she call the fire department or something? She breathed in the aroma of the woodland, so fresh and sweet, remembering it all too clearly. The crackle of flames, the acrid smell of smoke, and most of all... the gripping fear. Shivering involuntarily, she placed her toe into the stirrup, sprang nimbly up onto Sunny's broad back and settled herself down into the saddle.

"Believe me," she announced determinedly. "There really was a fire," then she turned toward her companion with a smile, trying to focus on some thing else. "Do you live near here?"

Bess nodded, waving her hand vaguely toward the woodland behind them.

"Just over that way. I live with my dad... My Mom died when I was two."

Memories of the fire faded. "Oh... I mean... I am so sorry."

"Don't be," she shrugged. "It was a long time ago, and I can't really remember her. Anyway, we do all right, my dad and me... except that he's away a lot, but I'm used to looking after myself."

She scrambled onto Domino's broad back from a tree stump beside the pathway, wriggled into position and dug her heels into his broad rib cage. He shambled into a reluctant jog trot to keep up with the big dun gelding's swinging walk, and for a few minutes the two girls rode in silence, breathing in the heady aroma of the woodland as they re-lived the heart stopping moment on the pathway. Tilly was the first to break the heavy silence.

"We could have been killed if you hadn't been so brave."
"Well, you weren't," laughed Bess. "So forget about that and concentrate on your plan to save Sunny."

Tilly's heart tightened. "We can do it, can't we?" she murmured.

"No… *You* are going to do it," declared Bess. "I'm just pointing you in the right direction."

"But you *are* going to come with me…"

Her voice tailed off. "Well, at least tell me more about this Cricklewood place."

"Only if you wait for me," grumbled Bess. Her voice wobbled slightly with the effort of trying to sit bareback to Domino's bouncy trot, and Tilly reined in, slowing her horse's eager walk until the cob came alongside.

It was tight for two on the narrow pathway, and the girls' attention was taken at first by trying to stop the horses from nibbling at each other. Eventually Tilly gave an exasperated sigh and drew ahead.

"So come on," she cried, twisting around in the saddle. "Tell me all about Cricklewood Farm."

"Well," began Bess. "It's not very far. You turn right when you leave the wood and then take the next right up a long narrow lane. You can see the house from the main road; it's right up on top of the hill. The couple that have it are called… Oh, I can't remember." She drew her thick dark eyebrows into a frown. "Atkins, that's it, their name is Atkins. Anyway, they are young and they haven't been there very long, but the good thing is that they must like horses because they have two of their own."

A drum began beating inside Tilly's chest as hope soared. "What are they like… have you seen them?"

Bess grinned. "Seen who? The Atkinses or their horses?"

"Either!" cried Tilly.

"Well I've only seen the horses a couple of times when

22

I've ridden past the farm. They're usually in the field right by the lane. They certainly seem to be well enough looked after. One is a little chestnut Arab mare and the other looks like an old hunter. He's a big good-looking bay with a white star. I've never seem them being ridden, though."

"And what about the Atkinses?" cut in Tilly.

Domino chose that moment to dive into the grass, and Bess kicked him forward with a yell. She looked up, smiling broadly, her face pink with exertion.

"That is one of the bad things about owning a cob," she declared. "All he thinks about is food… a bit like me, really. How far off is supper time anyway?"

"It's hardly lunchtime yet," responded Tilly, glancing at her watch. To her surprise the hands pointed almost to five o' clock. She looked up, noting uneasily how low the sun hung in the sky and how the shadows were already lengthening. What was going on? Where had the day gone? A shiver ran down her spine.

"Tell me about the Atkinses," she pleaded urgently.

"Not much to tell," responded Bess. "I've never actually met them, just seen them around. But they seem nice, ordinary really. Come on, we're almost there, and I have to go."

She jumped down from Domino's broad back and looped the reins through her arm, looking up expectantly. Tilly pushed aside her sense of unease. It must be the shock, she decided, that made everything seem so… odd.

"It hardly seems like five minutes since breakfast," she announced, jumping lightly to the ground. Sunny pushed his face against her, real and solid and safe, making everything better.

"Well, it feels like supper time to me," declared Bess. "Don't worry, you'll easily find the farm."

"And I'll see you again…?"

Bess stepped forward, her jolly face suddenly serious.

"Of course," she said simply. "Anyway…" Her expression brightened. "You owe me one."

For a moment time seemed suspended. Tension crackled between them in an unbreakable bond, forged by the fear they had faced together.

"If you ever want anything," declared Tilly fiercely. "I mean… if you need me… just call. Anytime."

"Night or day?" smiled Bess.

"Night or day," promised Tilly.

A flush passed over her fair skin. She held out her hand and Bess took it, gripping it tightly for just a moment.

"Be careful," she warned with a twinkle in her eyes. "I might just hold you to that. See you soon."

"See you soon," echoed Tilly, turning Sunny's head toward home, and as he set off into an eager walk she glanced back, hand raised in farewell. The pathway behind them was silent and empty, different somehow. She shook her head. How had Bess and Domino disappear so quickly? They must have taken a shortcut though the trees.

Her breath sounded loud in her ears. The dense woodland loomed around her. Had there really been a fire in this silent, peaceful place? Doubt flooded in again, and with it a terrifying confusion. Suddenly she longed for open space. Sensing her mood, Sunny broke into an excited jog trot, sidling along the familiar pathway, forcing her attention away from thoughts that made her feel half crazy. She sat determinedly to his swinging gait, her fingers taut on the reins… listening with screaming senses to the hum of traffic as they approached the final corner.

The pathway widened. A shallow breath caught in her throat and her world closed in to one central point. For there, just ahead of them, tall and imposing against the silver gray ribbon of the road beyond, stood the ornate shape of the Millennium gate.

chapter three

Metal clanged against metal with echoing finality, and Tilly paused for a moment, staring up at the intricately woven arch above the gate. The numbers 2000 carefully forged in iron. How did they do that? How did they take a solid iron bar and twist it into something beautiful? Like magic. She had thought it was magic when they galloped around the corner to find that the gate was gone, but of course, now that she had it straight in her head it was so obvious. Crickle Wood was huge. They had simply strayed onto a similar pathway, one she had never been on before. Strange how your mind can play stupid tricks when you are in shock.

Sunny pushed his face against her and she rubbed his forehead, reluctantly remembering the terrifying moments when he had lost his head completely. Is it true that all horses really are still wild deep down, she wondered? He blew through his nostrils, grabbing greedily for grass, and a smile crept onto her face.

"There's certainly nothing wild about you now, boy," she announced with a sigh of relief. "Who would ever believe that you just almost got us both killed?"

Placing a toe in the stirrup, she hauled herself wearily up into the saddle and persuaded her suitably tamed mount to walk on. Traffic flashed by just ahead of them now, along the busy road. People intent upon getting there, wherever *there* was.

As normality filtered back Tilly's fears seemed a lifetime ago. All she really wanted now was to go home, but Bess's suggestion kept swirling around in her head. Should she try to find Cricklewood Farm right now, or was it too late in the day? Sunny's hooves made a squishing sound along the broad grass verge, and she peered ahead between his sharply pricked ears. First right along a narrow lane, wasn't it? Excitement bubbled, dispelling her lethargy.

The day seemed incredibly bright after the gloom of the woodland. Pale autumn sunshine bathed everything in its soft glow; turning dying brown leaves to red and gold. Tilly looked around uncertainly. The sun had seemed much lower before she left the wood. Way above her head a patch of blue miraculously appeared, dispelling the rumbling gray clouds, as she glanced uneasily at her watch. She had told Bess that it was almost five o' clock half an hour ago; what was she thinking? The fingers on her watch now pointed very definitely to two. It was still only two o' clock in the afternoon!

The hard muscle of Sunny's neck felt real and solid beneath her hand, comforting in the face of confusion.

"What a day, boy," she announced out loud. His wonderfully familiar ears flicked back as if in sympathy, and her words came out in a hurried jumble as she allowed herself to remember. "Getting lost in the first place was bad enough, and then the fire and the vanishing gate, but at least we made some new friends, and…" Hope flooded in, and she leaned forward, flinging her arms impulsively around his thick neck. "Perhaps we've even found a way for you to stay."

When he felt the reins loosen Sunny saw his opportunity and, totally unperturbed by his mistress's enthusiasm, he yanked his head down to grab a tasty morsel of grass. Tilly found herself hanging perilously forward in the direction of his ears, giggling furiously while trying to retrieve her balance, and totally unaware of the pickup truck that slid to a halt beside her.

"You OK, hon?"

A man's deep concerned voice brought her sharply back

upright, face crimson with effort and embarrassment. She gathered up the reins and nodded hurriedly.

"Yes… I mean." Sunny sidestepped, snorting at the vehicle. "Thank you… we're fine."

Bright blue eyes, narrowed against the sun that lent a golden gleam to lined and leathery skin met hers; and beyond she noticed his angular shape… a round face, soft contours, a gentle smile. Automatically Tilly found herself smiling back at the pleasant-faced woman in the passenger seat, and then with a brief lift of a hand they were gone and she was all alone again on the side of the busy road.

"Come on."

She picked up the reins and tightened her calves, suddenly sure. The sooner she found this Cricklewood Farm place, the sooner Sunny's future would be secure.

Tall hedges grew on either side of the narrow lane, untended, alive with wildlife and shimmering autumn colors. Tilly kept to the center. Sunny's feet thudding softly on the narrow strip of grass, clattering onto pavement as he spooked at an imaginary monster.

"There it is."

The sound of her own voice lent confidence, and she urged him into a gentle jog trot toward a half open, tilting wooden gate. Chickens were everywhere. The smell of them, the sound of them, squawking, clucking, cackling; it sounded to Tilly as if a million busy beaks were all trying to speak at once.

Beside the sad wooden gate was a lopsided sign. *CRICKLE-WOOD CHICKENS*. Sunny snorted at it, unnerved by the frenzied atmosphere. Tilly jumped to the ground, pulled his reins over his head and led him into what must have once been an orchard, carefully closing the rickety gate behind her before starting along a rough track. The grass around the ancient apple trees was made patchy and bare by scratching talons. Wooden chicken coops were dotted everywhere, as if flung down at

random, their sagging roofs a perfect perch for preening birds. Sunny sidetracked at every one, blowing through his nostrils at the strutting white chickens that seemed totally oblivious to the horse and rider, their bright beady eyes scouring the earth as they busily searched for anything edible. Just ahead of them a mottled, swaggering young rooster, pointed his sharp yellow beak to the ground before reaching skywards with red clad head. His cock-a-doodle cry rang out above the sound of busy birds, and a small flock ran toward him in ungainly fashion, wings flapping and necks outstretched. He scratched in the dirt, proudly showing his find, clucking an aggressive warning to a nearby crow before standing back to oversee his brood. The large crow cocked its head to one side, then stretched its blue black wings, flapping them slowly as it rose lazily up onto the fence. Tilly watched its progress with interest.

"This," she declared out loud, "is a very odd place."

"Not as odd as the folks who live here," came an unexpected answer from just behind her. Sunny, with his all-around vision, seemed unperturbed by the sudden appearance of a tall, broad shouldered, gangly figure, but Tilly's heart lurched with embarrassment. It had been one thing *thinking* about finding Cricklewood Farm but quite another actually asking for… for what?… a job?… a stable to lease? And after being caught putting the place down, what hope did she have now? Her tongue attached itself to the roof of her mouth and color flooded her face.

"I… I didn't mean it like that…" she stuttered.

The teenage lad ran a hand though his thick mop of hair and gave her a cockeyed smile.

"Like what?"

"I mean… I don't think it is odd… not really…"

"Yes you do."

He was awkward looking, with irregular, suntanned features a long way from being classically handsome. But his eyes

29

were kind, she decided, and somehow vaguely familiar. She tried again.

"It's just that I've never been to a chicken farm before."

"Well, if you had come in the front way you just might have been a bit more impressed," he told her with a broad grin. "Who are you looking for anyway, or do you want to buy some eggs?"

She glanced around uncertainly. There was the house, square and stone built, gray like the rest of the buildings in the area, and sure enough, she could see the back door.

"No... I mean I haven't come for eggs."

The mottled gray and white rooster chose that moment to run forward, lunging at the boy's Wellington boots, talons outstretched. The boy sidestepped, laughing.

"Roger hates me, I'm afraid," he explained apologetically. "I once accidentally stepped on one of his hens, and now he thinks I'm out to hurt them all."

"I didn't know roosters had attitude," giggled Tilly, stepping back nervously as the large bird flew toward him again, feathers ruffled angrily and wings outstretched. She looked on anxiously as the boy pushed the bird away with his foot and turned toward her with an easy grin.

"Come on," he suggested. "Let's get away from him."

Roger followed them for a few yards, squawking noisily, before losing interest, and the boy glanced across at Tilly with a twinkle in his bright blue eyes.

"That's more like it. We don't really keep roosters, but Dad has a soft spot for Roger. He's allowed to roam around wherever he wants with his flock in tow."

"But where do they sleep and where do they lay their eggs?" asked Tilly, intrigued by the fact that chickens actually appeared to have their own characters. They were, after all, something completely new to her. As far as she was concerned eggs came off supermarket shelves and chickens came frozen. The thought made her feel sick.

"I'm sorry," she said, changing the subject. "My name is Matilda, Matilda McCloud, but you can call me Tilly."

"And I'm Dillon, you can call me Dillon, and now you can tell me why you're here."

Why was she here? Nerves fluttered inside her stomach.

"This is Sunny," she mumbled, patting the gelding's golden brown neck. "Do you like horses?"

"I like all animals, but I can't say that I have ever had much to do with horses," remarked Dillon. He reached out tentatively to touch his velvety nose. "But he looks nice. Very spirited."

A concentrated frown clouded Tilly's face as she tried to think of the right thing to say.

"I suppose you work here…"

Dillon laughed. "Well, as I live here and there's always loads of work to do I don't really have much choice. There's just me and my Mom and Dad, you see… Actually…" color flooded his face and he cleared his throat. "What I really want to do when I leave school is to train as a vet…"

He hesitated, gauging Tilly's reaction before going on.

"My dad wants me to stay here, though, and help to run the place… take over one day, I suppose."

"Have you told him?"

At Tilly's pointed question he shrugged, and his momentary lapse into seriousness was replaced once again by a happy-go-lucky smile.

"You should," she advised. Her brain was ticking overtime, trying to slot Dillon into the information passed on to her by Bess.

"So… if your parents own this place then your name must be Atkins?"

He nodded half-heartedly, his mind still full of dreams.

"But I thought the Atkins couple were young, and I thought that they had horses of their own."

31

"Well you thought wrong," he declared. "My Mom used to ride but that was a long time ago."

"And they're not young?" cut in Tilly.

"Definitely not young," he laughed. "Anyway…"

He turned toward the house, hand shading his forehead. "Here they are now. See for yourself."

They walked along the side of the house; Sunny's hooves clip-clopping now on pavement, around the corner to where a vehicle was driving in through newly painted white gates.

"Told you it was better looking around the front," remarked Dillon.

The surrounding paddocks were still littered with chicken coops, wire mesh and fluttering, clucking birds, noted Tilly, but the garden in front of the house was neat and tidy and the yard was swept clean.

"It's very nice, and I…"

Her voice faded out as she recognized the vehicle that rumbled to a halt outside the front door.

"Is this your mom and dad?"

"You don't need to look so scared," grinned Dillon. "They're not that bad."

"No… I mean…we've met already."

The driver's door of the battered white pickup opened and a tall man disentangled himself from the vehicle. Tilly's gaze met the startling blue eyes she had seen in the lane, Dillon's eyes.

"Bob Atkins," he said with a broad smile, holding out his hand. Tilly took it, wincing as he squeezed her fingers and pumped them up and down enthusiastically.

"And I'm Vee."

A small, rounded woman, with a lovely clear complexion and gentle eyes, came around the side of the pickup carrying two bulging plastic bags.

"Lovely horse," she remarked, nodding toward Sunny who

stood quietly for once, surveying his surroundings with obvious approval. Then she placed her bags on the front doorstep, walked confidently toward him and ran her hand down his neck, allowing him to snuffle against her pockets.

"Well, I think so," agreed Tilly. "In fact…"

Her tongue seemed too big for her mouth and the words stuck somewhere inside her head.

"In fact what…?" asked Vee Atkins. "Come on, we're not that scary, you know. Just tell us what's on your mind."

The words came out in a torrent.

"I wondered if you had any jobs going anything will do I just need somewhere to keep Sunny he's going to be sold you see because my mom and dad are…"

The words dried up as quickly as they had escaped and she looked at the ground, face burning as her hopes slowly began to fade.

"Well, we've no horse work here," remarked Vee. "But if you don't mind getting dirty there are always jobs to do."

She glanced across at her husband and the creases across his forehead deepened for a moment.

"Dillon," he barked. "Why don't you go with…?" He looked at Tilly, eyebrows raised.

"Matilda," she told him. "Matilda McCloud, but everyone calls me Tilly."

"Well, Matilda everyone calls me Tilly McCloud," he smiled. "Why don't you go with Dillon everyone calls me Dillon and put this magnificent horse of yours into the barn, then come inside for a drink and we'll talk about it."

Tilly felt as if she was walking on air. *We'll talk about it*, Bob Atkins had said. That meant that there really was hope… didn't it?

"Well, you look a bit happier," remarked Dillon with the crooked grin she was becoming quite used to.

"I'll be happier still if your parents really do let Sunny stay here." Tilly's cheeks flamed. What if she had gotten it completely wrong? "I mean... well… Is that what they meant, do you think?" she mumbled.

Dillon shrugged.

"Who knows? We could certainly use some help, and we do have a stable – well, a kind of pen in the barn, actually, but it's big enough for a horse. He'll have to like chickens, of course."

"I think anyone who comes here would have to like chickens," grinned Tilly.

"And what about roosters?" Dillon opened his startling blue eyes very wide and gave an exaggerated shiver. "Mmm… well Roger needs someone new to chase. Why else would we consider letting you stay… and why do you think the last girl left?"

Tilly laughed, digging him in the ribs.

"I'm not afraid of a stupid rooster," she exclaimed.

"Well, you should be afraid… be very afraid," cried Dillon in a high-pitched, quivery voice.

Emotion flooded over Tilly, leaving her strangely wobbly and weak. What was happening to her? Here she was, on the verge of saving Sunny, and all the fears of the day seemed to be rushing back in. It had nothing to do with Dillon's crazy threats about Roger, she knew that, it was just a kind of delayed reaction. It was easy to be brave when you had to be, but now, when everything seemed as if it just might be working out… An image of Bess's dark eyes flashed into her mind and she found herself longing for the company of her newfound friend.

"Look…" Dillon's attempt at a scary face puckered into one of concern. "I didn't really mean it, you know. Roger is just a pussy cat…"

Something gurgled in Tilly's throat. The thought of Roger as a pussycat suddenly seemed so ridiculously funny. The gurgle in her throat bubbled out into slightly hysterical laughter and

34

she tried desperately to pull herself together before Dillon had her pegged as a complete idiot.

"I'm not usually like this," she explained apologetically, wiping her damp eyes. "It's just…"

"Just what?" Dillon took a firm hold of Sunny's rein as they reached the wooden door of a large stone barn and, placing a sympathetic hand on her shoulder, he turned her around to face him. "You don't fool me, you know. What is it that has upset you so much, or is it just that you're worried about your horse and your parents?"

"Something like that," muttered Tilly. "And… and there was a fire in the woods. It panicked Sunny and he bolted. If it hadn't been for Bess we'd have ended up in a pile up on the main road."

"Had somebody left the gate open?"

Confusion flooded over her.

"We were on a different path," she whispered, looking up at him. "There was no gate."

For a moment Dillon held her gaze before dispelling the doubt in his face with a quick, broad grin.

"Must have missed that one," he remarked. "And I don't know anyone called Bess… But I suppose if you had strayed right to the other side of the woods…"

"Yes," cried Tilly. "That was it. He bolted, you see, right through a really overgrown part." She shivered again, closing her eyes against the memories that flooded in.

"Well, I certainly believe you about the fire," exclaimed Dillon, pointing to Sunny's flank. Tilly shrank back in horror at the sight of an ugly scorch mark on his smooth golden coat.

"Hey!" He gave her shoulder a quick squeeze. "It's nothing, just surface hair. Weird though, I can't ever remember there ever being a fire in the woods before. Anyway, there's always a first time, and all's well that ends well. You are OK now, so let's just go and show Sunny his stable."

"*His* stable," breathed Tilly, all thoughts of fires and bolting horses suddenly erased. "Do you really mean that?"

"Well, we'll have to check with my mom and dad, of course," Dillon reminded her. "But it does sound as if they *might* let him stay. You'll have to work, you know."

"I'll do anything," cried Tilly. "Anything at all."

The stable in the barn was more than adequate, decided Tilly. In fact Sunny dived into the full hayrack right away and seemed intrigued by the two Jersey cows in the next stall.

"They're called Bluebell and Daffodil," Dillon informed her, scratching their heads. "My Mom loves spring flowers, and she tries to name all the animals after them. Even the pig is called Primrose; she's just a pet. We keep the cows for their milk, though; well, at least Bluebell gives milk, but Daffodil is dry at the moment. Sunny seems to like them well enough, anyway."

"Do you really think your mom and dad will let him stay?" asked Tilly eagerly. It really did seem just too good to be true.

"Well, come on, let's go and find out," he suggested.

Together they walked across the yard and through the open front door. The house smelled of food and chickens and cows, so many unfamiliar scents. Tilly wrinkled her nose, determined to like everything about Cricklewood Farm.

"You'll get used to it," Dillon assured her. "Give you a month and you'll love the chickens as much as we do."

"I will if they help me to keep Sunny," she agreed. Dillon ran his fingers through his red brown hair. "I don't think anyone *could* split you two up," he remarked, raising one eyebrow.

"Just let them try," cried Tilly ferociously as they burst in through the kitchen door. The scent of fresh baked bread made her stop in her tracks, inhaling deeply.

"Straight from the oven," announced Vee Atkins, placing a

crusty loaf on the large wooden table. "Sit down, the pair of you, and I'll butter you a slice. Tea or juice?"

Tilly sipped her freshly squeezed orange juice, fingers wrapped around the glass, clinging to it as she longed to cling to this special place that Bess had led her to. She waited, adrenalin making her nerve ends tingle as Dillon asked the question for her.

"So, Dad… Mom… what do you think?"

Bob Atkins smiled, the same crooked smile as his son, and his piercing blue eyes twinkled from their background of tanned leathery skin.

"About what?" he drawled, concentrating all his attention on buttering a thick slice of fresh bread and spreading it with homemade strawberry jam.

"Don't keep the poor girl in suspense," chided his wife, her gentle eyes turned toward Tilly. He looked up at her, slamming his fist down onto the table as if to make an announcement, and she felt her stomach churn.

"That's a good sign," advised Dillon. "I think it means Sunny can stay."

"Can he… please … I'll work every day."

Vee Atkins pursed her lips, trying, impossibly, to look stern. "Not on school days, I hope," she remarked, with a barely concealed smile. Sensing success, Tilly's face brightened.

"After school," she cried eagerly. "I could work *after* school."

Bob Atkins rapped on the table again, with his fingers this time. "Right," he announced. "I'll tell you what we'll do…"

All eyes turned toward him and Tilly felt suddenly sick. She placed her half eaten crust of bread back onto the plate and twirled her empty glass around between her shaking fingers.

"The horse can stay here, but you'll work for his keep. You can use the stable in the barn and turn him out in the paddock at the end of the lane. We will provide hay, feed and bedding,

37

and on school days one of us will feed him for you and turn him out – as long as you come up later to muck him out and bring him in, that is. Or do you keep him out all the time?"

"Either… anything… whatever…"

Excitement was like a living thing, taking over Tilly's whole being. It was a dream, she decided. It had to be a dream.

"Well… which is it?"

Bob Atkins eyes were narrowed. Was that doubt she could see in his eyes? Was he regretting his offer already?

"Whatever is best for you," she stuttered.

He nodded brusquely. "You will have to work, of course. You know, earn his keep. Weekends, holidays… It'll be hard work, and if you don't live up to your end of the bargain the deal is off."

"And you'll need your parents' approval, of course," reminded Vee.

Tilly felt her head nodding uncontrollably as elation flooded through her veins. An image of Bess's dark, serious eyes, flashed into her mind. It was all thanks to that chance meeting in the woods. If there hadn't been a fire, if Sunny hadn't bolted, if Bess hadn't been so brave… It didn't bear thinking about. Bess had probably saved both their lives, and now she had saved Sunny from being sold. She had go and find her again, had to thank her."

"So go home, see what your parents say, and let us know…"

Tilly stared vacantly at Vee who was looking at her with a curious expression on her face.

"Yes," she cried, tears lighting up her deep blue eyes. "Thank you so much. I'll go home and see my Mom right now."

Tilly twisted around to wave goodbye to Dillon as she rode off along the lane – through the front entrance this time. He felt like a friend already. From having no real friends at all since moving to Millside cottage, today she had made two. It

38

felt good, she decided. Perhaps she could take Dillon to meet Bess… but not the first time. She and her newfound friend had too much emotion to relive, too many memories to relate. Oh how she wished the sturdy dark-haired girl were here now, to share her relief about Sunny's future. Her chest grew tight as she thought about the whole traumatic experience of the day, and suddenly it seemed difficult to breathe. Images flashed into her mind, clear and vivid. Flickering flames, sparks showering down like golden rain, and hooves, galloping, out of control toward… She closed her eyes, forcing the memories out of her head. It was over, they were safe, and now she had to think of the future.

"Come on, boy," she urged, taking comfort from the solid feel of the horse beneath her. Sunny pricked his ears and broke into trot. Yesterday seemed such a long time ago, today was one for the record books, and tomorrow… A warm glow spread through her whole body making toes and fingers tingle. Tomorrow beckoned enticingly.

chapter four

Tilly closed Sunny's stable door, slid the bolt carefully and stood for a moment, watching him dive into his feed. This, hopefully, was to be his last night at Burnbrook stables and she wouldn't be sorry to leave. Roland Cuthbert, the pompous, old-fashioned ex military man who owned it, ruled with an iron rod. His wife, who did most of the work, was quiet and unapproachable, a miserable person, Tilly had decided – and who wouldn't be, being married to RC? Most of the other horse owners who stabled there were adults, who had full board because they were working during the day, so their paths rarely crossed, and when she did occasionally see them at weekends they were always polite but very distant. She had felt like an intruder ever since Sunny arrived at the stables.

Fortunately it was almost the end of the month – her board was paid up until the day after tomorrow, so there was nothing to stop her from leaving right away. Excitement bubbled at the thought. Of course she still had to tell the Cuthberts... what if they insisted on a month's notice? Could they do that? As soon as the idea flashed into her mind, anxiety set in. Perhaps she should go and see them right now, prepare them, so to speak... But she hadn't told her mother yet.

She stood for a moment longer, watching Sunny munch contentedly. What if he missed the company of other horses when he went to live at Cricklewood Farm? An image of his two future stable companions flashed into her mind, Bluebell and Daffodil.

"You'll have to make do with cows now," she told him with a smile. He blew hard down his nostrils, tossing his head. "And chickens," she added turning away. Suddenly the future looked so much more hopeful.

Roland Cuthbert's rotund figure approached from the direction of the house just as she lifted the latch on the yard gate. A sigh escaped her and her stomach churned. What did *he* want? Should she just tell him now and be done with it?

"Good news," he called, puffing slightly as he increased his pace to catch up with her before she left. His tweed jacket flapped as he trotted toward her, and his face seemed to be gradually turning an alarming shade of pink. "I've got…"

He stopped in front of her, leaning forward for a moment to catch his breath, hands firmly fixed on the front of his thighs.

"Your mother said…"

He stood up straight, painstakingly fastening the buttons on his jacket…

"That you…"

Damping his fingers he smoothed down his generously proportioned moustache.

"Yes…?" enquired Tilly impatiently.

"A buyer," he exclaimed with delight, brushing himself down. "I've found you a buyer!"

Her eyes darkened momentarily, and then her face paled as the truth dawned. Roland Cuthbert had found someone who wanted to buy Sunny.

She stared at him, wide eyed.

"But…!"

He smiled happily.

"They called in to see him yesterday when you were at school, and he rang back with a decision just ten minutes ago."

"But…" blurted out Tilly. "They haven't even ridden him."

"Didn't need to," he barked. "You did that for them. They saw the horse at the pony club show you took him to last month."

"He refused at the first fence," remembered Tilly, her heart racing in panic.

"Potential!" cried Roland with great delight. "That's what it's all about."

She stood her ground, collecting her thoughts, anger bubbling through the awesome panic.

"I've changed my mind."

There, she had said it. Her confidence grew.

"In fact I'm afraid that this will be Sunny's last day here. I'm sorry it's such short notice, but I found somewhere else for him and… well… we just can't afford it here."

Her appealing gaze fell upon stony ground as Roland Cuthbert saw his hopes of a sale disappear.

"Ten per cent," he yelled. "Your mother promised me ten per cent. I've spent time and effort on this sale…"

Tilly looked on alarmed as his already crimson face turned a deep shade of fuchsia.

"I'm sorry," she murmured, wondering if she should go and call for his wife. He pulled himself up to his full height, running his fingers over his moustache.

"I will be paid," he yelled. "And I'm going to call your mother right now, young lady. I think you'll find that she can be persuaded to keep her word."

"He's my horse," cried Tilly, remembering Bess's advice. Roland Cuthbert's only response was to stamp off across the immaculate concrete yard.

"And I'll be taking him away tomorrow," she reminded him.

"We'll see about that," was his parting shot.

Tilly felt as if someone was twisting a knife in her guts. She tried to imagine Bess's brave face; what would *she* do in this situation? The answer was there at once.

Fight, of course. Stick up for your rights. Her determined

42

voice rang in Tilly's ears, and she pushed back her shoulders, allowing the gate to slam shut behind her. No one was going to take Sunny away from her… however much they were prepared to pay.

Fenna McCloud rummaged frantically through the drawer, her pale face flushed with exertion as she threw item after item out onto the floor. For a moment she paused to run her hand through her thick fair hair, blinking away the tears that threatened. Where was it?

"What are you doing?"

Tilly's voice made her start. She paused, hands outstretched, guilt plainly etched on her drawn features.

"You've spoken to RC," declared her daughter in a cold, flat voice. "What did he say to you?"

Fenna's face crumpled.

"He…I mean… I was just looking for the boarding contract," she admitted.

Tilly stared hard at the floor, clinging on to her self-control.

"So I suppose he told you, then?"

"In no uncertain terms," responded Fenna with the ghost of a smile. Tilly looked up, her eyes shining with tears.

"Oh, Mom," she blurted out. "I know I've been selfish and unsupportive. I want to help, honestly I do, but… well… there has to be another way…"

She drew herself up to her full height, deep blue eyes so wide with passion that they seemed to take over all of her face.

"I can't sell Sunny. He *is* my horse after all, and anyway I've found somewhere else to keep him, somewhere where it won't cost you a penny."

For a moment they stared at each other, so alike and yet so far apart. Fenna was the first to crumble.

"Oh, sweetheart, I am so sorry."

She placed her hands over her face, long fair hair falling forward, and Tilly felt a sharp pain swell inside her as she remembered Bess's words. *Your mother must be so angry and confused.* All *Tilly* had done through the trauma of her father leaving was to think about herself.

"No..." she cried, swiftly closing the gap between them. "It's me who should be sorry."

For a while they stood quite still, arms around each other, until Fenna pulled back and gently wiped away her daughter's tears. It was such a relief to have her mother back, decided Tilly. For weeks now she felt as if she had been living with a stranger, but perhaps it was she who had been the stranger.

"I can't let Sunny go, Mom," she announced with quiet determination. "I know that all I've done up to now is to whine about everything, and I haven't been any support to you, but it's going to be different from now on. I'm going to fight to keep him... you'll see... and work hard."

"Well, then... you'd better fill me in on this place you've found," suggested her mother with a weary smile.

"And you'd better tell me exactly what RC said," responded Tilly.

They found the missing contract in with a jumble of insurance documents.

"I really am going to have to have a sort out," cried Fenna. "It's just that your dad..."

"I know," finished Tilly. "He used to deal with all that kind of thing. Well I'm here to help now. We can do it together."

"When we've sorted out this thing with Roland Cuthbert," sighed Fenna. "Now let me see... he told me that in the contract it said a month's notice was required or else an extra month's payment became due."

"And can he do that?" cried Tilly. "Can he make us pay for something we haven't had?"

Fenna scoured the contract, eyes narrowed.

"It all depends what we signed our names to," she said. "After all… to be fair."

She looked up at her daughter with a troubled frown. "If we had given him a month's notice then he could have found another boarder to take our place, couldn't he? So in a way he *is* losing out. And then there's the sale. He's obviously put time and effort into it."

For the first time, reluctantly, Tilly saw Roland Cuthberts's side of things.

"Can he force us to keep our word… you know… make us sell?"

"Oh, no!" Her mother was adamant. "Sunny belongs to us… or… as you pointed out… to you. You haven't signed anything, so it's just his word against yours."

"And what does the contract say?"

Tilly was on tenterhooks as she waited for her mother's response.

"He's right," said Fenna quietly. "That is exactly what the contract says."

For a moment they both just stared at the neatly typed words, as though expecting them to miraculously change.

"Well there's only one thing to do!"

Tilly stood up tall, suddenly decided and totally resolute. "I am going to have to throw myself on his mercy."

"If anyone is going to see Roland then I think it should be me," insisted Fenna. "I'll go tomorrow, tell him the truth, and hope that I can talk him into being lenient with us… now come on." She looked at her daughter as if determined to rise above the depression that had been haunting her. "You had better tell me what you've been up to."

Tilly left nothing out. By the time she had finished telling her mother all about the fire and Bess and Cricklewood Farm Fenna McCloud's gray eyes were wide with horror.

"I can't believe that you've just been through all that while I was having a boring ordinary day at work," she cried. "I don't think I'd better let you go out riding on your own ever again."

Tilly simply shrugged and let out a long, drawn sigh. Her experience in the woods had been terrifying at the time but, since then, other things had slightly overshadowed it – the wonders of Cricklewood Farm, for instance, and the awful revelation that taking Sunny away from Burnbrook might not be as simple as she had at first imagined. She blinked hard and forced a bright smile onto her face.

"How could anyone have a boring, ordinary day when they work in a nursery school?" she exclaimed. "And as for not letting me go riding on my own… well, let's just hope that I'm still able to when Roland Cuthbert has finished with us."

Her mother's face fell.

"I'm sorry, love," she murmured. "I should never have told him to sell Sunny in the first place, however desperate I was. Not without your permission. I'll go and see him after work tomorrow and try to sort something out."

Disappointment flooded over Tilly like a great black cloud.

"But I'm supposed to take Sunny to Cricklewood Farm tomorrow," she cried. Fenna smiled, a worried kind of smile, and gave her daughter a quick hug.

"One more day won't make any difference, surely," she insisted. "And your board is paid for tomorrow anyway. Now come on; early to bed for you, I think. Things will look better in the morning."

The night was so black that when Tilly opened her eyes it was as if she was still sleeping. For a moment panic held her in its fierce grip, and then suddenly a chink of light appeared and she was able to breathe once again. Air rushed into her lungs with a hiss. In her dreams she had been back in Crickle Wood with the crackle of flames in her ears, galloping hooves pounding through her whole being, a silent scream welling inside her. But in the moment before the scream broke loose from its confines, in the self same moment that she heard a distant, haunting cry, she opened her eyes to the blackness. Day or night... night or day, both became one and the same. That was what Bess had said, she remembered. *Any time... night or day.* "Night or day," she had responded.

The moon slipped from behind a cloud and pale light filtered through her window, bringing clarity. Her jumbled thoughts became suddenly clear. Sunny; he was her only concern. He was the one she had to watch out for. She couldn't wait all day for her mother to sort it out. This was something she had to do for herself.

She slipped from beneath the cozy warmth of her comforter, shivering slightly. Her alarm clock shone out into the room... 6:30 a.m., plenty of time... plenty of time for what?

"To go and see Roland Cuthbert," she murmured, answering her own unspoken question. Her teeth clamped tight shut and she took a deep breath. "I can persuade him to see reason, I know I can."

She was gone from the house long before her mother woke, slipping silently from the warmth of the kitchen into the sharp crispness of the autumn morning, shoulders hunched and fists pushed down hard into the pockets of her quilted jacket. It normally took her only ten minutes to get to Burnbrook stables; she made it in five, muscles and chest aching with effort. For a moment she paused, hands pressed down onto her knees as apprehension struck. What if she

47

couldn't talk him around? What if there was a way that he could force her to sell Sunny?

The lights were already on in the house, warm and yellow, comforting, approachable. If only Roland Cuthbert was the same. She faltered – go now, or after she had mucked out? Now, she decided, jutting out her chin.

Maggie Cuthbert was in the kitchen. Tilly could see her through the window, singing as she washed the breakfast dishes. That was a good sign. Her knuckles hurt as she rapped them against the door.

"Come in," called Maggie brightly, and Tilly stepped into the cozy warmth of the kitchen, squirming uncomfortably at the sight of her muddy boots on the newly washed floor. Awkwardly she pulled them off and placed them out on the step.

"Sorry about that," she mumbled. "I'll wipe it up."

"No matter," insisted Maggie. Her voice was so cheerful that for a moment it threw Tilly's thoughts off track; she was more used to her being distant or even irritable, but definitely not bright and breezy.

"Are you looking for Roland?" she asked. "Well, you'll be pleased to know that you'll find him in a particularly good mood this morning… In fact…" Her eyes shone, lighting up her plain face, and she lifted her hands to her chest, twisting her fingers together. "Well, I suppose you might as well be the first to know…"

She held the moment, savoring it, her face pink with contained excitement.

"We have come into some money, and all our troubles are over."

Tilly just stared at her, unsure of how she should react.

"I didn't know you had any troubles," she eventually managed.

Maggie raised her eyebrows and rolled her eyes.

"Troubles! I can tell you something about troubles. Have you ever tried making money out of a stable yard? Anyway, now we don't have to any more."

"What! You're closing Burnbrook down?"

Things were moving way too fast for Tilly to take in. She felt a sense of relief when Maggie shook her head.

"Oh, no!" she exclaimed. "Well at least not for a while yet. It's just that an elderly relative of mine, Robert Malone, has died and left us quite an inheritance. We haven't seen him for years as he moved away after his daughter was killed. Anyway, it looks as if I am his only living relative."

"Well, I'm very happy for you," announced Tilly, meaning it. After all, the Cuthbert's good fortune could mean that Roland might be persuaded to be lenient with her about Sunny.

As soon as she walked into the murky, immaculate recess of his office Tilly knew that for once she was in luck. In fact everything seemed to be going so much her way lately that she found it just the teeniest bit scary. He turned toward her with a broad, unfamiliar smile on his face.

"I suppose you've come to apologize," he barked.

Tilly stared at the ground for a moment, her eyes firmly fastened on a worn patch in the red and gray carpet.

"I'm sorry that I didn't give you more notice about Sunny," she eventually blurted out. "And..."

She looked up at him appealingly.

"Well, to be honest, we just can't afford to pay the board any more. My dad has gone abroad to work and my Mom does her best, but – that's why she told you to sell him, you see, because she was desperate – but she had no right. Sunny belongs to me and I will never sell him."

She lifted her chin and met Roland Cuthbert's steely gray gaze full on.

"If I owe you money then I will work it off somehow," she promised. "But I have to take Sunny away today because it's the end of the month and we just can't afford to pay you any more money."

Her resolve faded as he narrowed his eyes, and her heart thudded so loudly in her chest that it seemed to fill the whole room.

"Well, young lady," he bellowed. "You have caught me in a very good mood today. Yesterday I would have had to insist that you kept to our deal, but for once I find myself prepared to be lenient. That doesn't mean that I don't expect you to make some payment, of course. I shall contact you when we're busy and you can work off the extra month's board… and *you* will have to call Charlie Montrose and tell him that you no longer wish to sell your horse. Here…" He scribbled a number down on a piece of paper and handed it to her. "And you'd better do it right now. You can use my phone."

With a curt nod he walked out of the room leaving Tilly staring at the old fashioned telephone, her nerve ends tingling. Tentatively she began to dial.

Although obviously disappointed Charles Montrose was very understanding about Tilly's situation. After promising to give him first refusal if she ever did decide to sell, she replaced the receiver with a thud, and elation flooded in. It was going to happen, it really was. Sunny was going to Cricklewood Farm.

Half an hour later Tilly piled her possessions into a meager pile for her mother to pick up later. Two buckets, half a bag of horse and pony mix, a fork, a skip and a grooming box. She stared at the items for a moment. What had she forgotten? Surely this couldn't be everything. Sunny tossed his head impatiently, and she reached up to run her hand down his neck.

"Time to go, boy," she murmured. A mass of butterflies fluttered inside her stomach. What if she was doing the wrong thing? There again, what did it matter anyway, since she had no other choice?

She placed her foot in the stirrup and swung up into the saddle, almost losing her balance when Sunny jumped sideways just as she sat down.

"Sorry," called Maggie Cuthbert from the direction of the barn. "I didn't mean to startle him."

For a moment Tilly saw the middle aged woman with new eyes; shoulders rounded by years of toil, tousled gray hair – long neglected by any hairdresser – blowing untidily around her prematurely lined face.

"Bye," she called with a sudden rush of happiness at the poor woman's good fortune. "I hope everything goes OK for you."

Maggie nodded in response, her tired features lighting up with an unaccustomed smile.

"Oh, I think it will now," she exclaimed. "I still can't quite believe it… although of course it is terrible for poor Robert."

She hesitated for a moment, color flooding her face as she remembered that her gain meant his loss, and then with a quick lift of her hand she headed for the house without a backward glance. Tilly sighed and gathered up the reins.

"Come on, boy," she urged, excitement kicking in. Sunny was all too happy to oblige. His hooves clattered on the pavement, his tail waved behind him like a banner, and elation rushed through her veins as she headed him out of the gate and off in the direction of his new home.

chapter five

Tilly rode through the front gates of Cricklewood Farm, confidence waning. The back entrance had been far less imposing. What if the Atkinses had changed their minds? What if they didn't like her? What if they didn't have the right feed for Sunny? So many what ifs… Too many what ifs…perhaps she should just scrap the whole idea.

"Well, you made it."

The familiar, friendly tone of Dillon's voice made her feel slightly better, but still she returned his broad grin with a worried frown.

"I hope I'm doing the right thing," she declared.

"Too late for second thoughts now," he laughed, taking Sunny's rein. "The stable is all ready, and we've even been out to get some horse feed for you. Come on, let's get him settled and I'll give you a proper tour of the place."

Fifteen minutes later Tilly heaved her saddle onto the rack by the barn door, placed her bridle carefully onto the hook beneath it, and went back across to take yet another look at her precious horse. He stood knee deep in straw, nostrils flaring as he surveyed his new surroundings with huge amber eyes.

"You are like a hen," announced Dillon, following her. "A fussy little broody hen."

"There's no one else to look out for him," she responded, leaning her elbows on the top rail of the large pen that acted as a stable. "He's got loads of room anyway. He'll like that."

"And two new friends to keep him company," he reminded her. "Do you think he's going to like them too?"

"Well, he seemed to get along with them well enough yesterday," she replied with a worried frown.

The two Jersey cows stared at Sunny with interest, lowing their greeting before reaching out toward him with long rough tongues. He stretched his neck tentatively in their direction, closer and closer, intrigued by his new companions until their tongues made contact with the tip of his velvety nose, then he leaped back with surprise to stare at them disdainfully from the back of his stable.

Tilly laughed. "You'd better get to know them, boy," she told him. "They are your new best friends."

He snorted his reply with a vigorous shake of his head and marched across to make a grab at his bulging hay net.

"See," announced Dillon proudly. "I told you we had everything ready."

Tilly felt a kind of glow ripple through her whole body. "Sorry for being a bit doubtful," she said. "It's just…"

"I know," he responded. "Come on – I'll show you around."

Tilly's feet dragged on the pedals as her legs churned their way up the final hill. The sign swung in front of her, *CRICKLEWOOD CHICKENS*. Was it really only a week since she had left Burnbrook to bring Sunny to this strange but friendly place? It felt like a lifetime. A lifetime since she said good bye to Maggie Cuthbert, a lifetime since she last saw Bess... Bess! A whole week had gone by and she still hadn't had time to look for her... but what a week. Rising at six to bike to Cricklewood Farm, mucking out, feeding, turning Sunny out into the meadow, and then biking home again to have a quick shower and change before racing out for the school bus. Yesterday it had had to wait while she ran down the lane, pink-cheeked and embarrassed as she scrambled aboard to hoots of laughter.

"Come on, chicken girl," Timmy Thwaites had yelled, and then everyone had started making clucking sounds. She had wished in that moment that the ground would open up and swallow her, but it was all worth it just to see Sunny so happy and content in his new home.

Above her head the sign swung, creaking gently in the sharp autumn breeze. She stepped off her bike with shaking legs and took a few gulps of air before lying it against a low stone wall just inside the newly painted white gate.

"Morning," called Bob Atkins as she headed for the barn. "I could feed him and put him out for you in the morning, you know… if it gets a bit too much…"

She nodded, smiling broadly. "Thanks, but he's my responsibility and you've done enough already."

"Well, if you're ever late or ill or anything, just give me a call," he told her, turning to watch his son's tall, lanky figure approaching from the direction of the house. "And I'll get Dillon to do it."

"Do what?" came the immediate reply. Bob merely laughed and disappeared in the direction of the long wooden chicken hut that housed his best layers.

Tilly answered the question for him.

"Your dad says that you will see to Sunny for me," she told him, withholding a smile. To her surprise Dillon grinned affably and nodded.

"I don't mind. I'm getting really fond of him, and after all…"

He looked at her with the shy, awkward smile that made him look sometimes like a huge, overgrown ten-year-old.

"I need experience with as many animals as I can if I'm going to be a vet one day."

Tilly clasped her hands tightly together.

"So you've told your dad then?"

Dillon concentrated hard on the ground in front of him.

"Well… not yet. Actually, there's something else I wanted to ask you."

"What?" urged Tilly. "What do you want to ask me?"

"Well…" He looked up at her appealingly. "I was hoping you might teach me to ride."

"Of course… Of course I will."

She stepped toward him eagerly, her face bright with delight. Here was something she could do to pay the Atkinses back for being so good to her.

"On Sunday," she told him. "I'll help out here in the morning and then I'll give you your first lesson."

It was only later, as she gave Sunny a quick brush, that she remembered. On Sunday she had intended to go back to Crickle Wood and look for Bess. She ran her hand over the rough scorch mark on his flank, her heart beating faster. How could she have forgotten her quest so easily, especially after last night when the memories had come back to haunt her again? She had wakened in the darkness, both shivering and sweating at the same time as the sound of crackling flames filled her ears, reliving the horror of Sunny's gallop toward catastrophe. And in the moment before sleep overtook her again, as tendrils of moonlight crept through her window, she had heard a faint and distant cry; just a whisper on the wind but a cry nevertheless, a cry for help. In her heart she had known that it was Bess who called out to her, and this morning, when she woke and it all seemed like a vague and distant dream, the compulsion to find her friend was so strong that she wanted to go to Crickle Wood there and then... How could she have forgotten so easily just because Dillon asked her for a riding lesson? Well, she would just have to go on Saturday, no matter what Bob Atkins said.

For a moment the thought of entering the cool darkness of the trees made her shiver. What if Sunny bolted again?

"It's half past seven, you know," called Vee Atkins from the direction of the back door. All thoughts of Bess and Crickle Wood vanished as panic set in, and with a hurried wave of thanks she raced for her bike. She was going to be late for the bus again!

Saturday dawned, bright and clear, a day to do things, she decided, as she ran down the stairs.

"Are you going to spend some time at home today?" called her mother from the bathroom.

She peered around the doorway. "Sorry Mom, no can do, I'm afraid. I have to earn Sunny's keep, remember."

Her mother sighed, a long drawn out sigh. "Well, I suppose it's better than being idle," she exclaimed. "But try not to be home too late. I hardly seem to have seen you this week."

This was to be her first proper day of working at Cricklewood Farm. Excitement bubbled inside her like a spring about to burst out of the ground. What would she have to do? She wondered. She found out just as soon as she had finished seeing to Sunny.

"Looks good, doesn't he?" remarked Dillon as they leaned side by side on the five-barred wooden gate. Tilly nodded enthusiastically, pride swelling inside her as she watched the golden dun gelding trotting off across the meadow, tail raised like a banner behind him and head held high.

"He's beautiful!" she sighed.

"About as beautiful as those lovely brown eggs that are waiting for you in the washhouse," interrupted Bob Atkins as he approached from the yard. "Come on, work to be done. Dillon will show you what to do."

After only half an hour Tilly was beginning to wish that she never had to look at an egg again. She broke two in the first five minutes much to Bob's annoyance.

"If you carry on like that you'll have to be paying me for Sunny's keep after all," he grumbled as she scooped the broken yolk into the bin.

After that she tried extra hard, placing each egg cautiously into the water and running her fingers over their smooth brown shells as gently as she could before placing them carefully into the waiting egg box.

"You'd think that they could find a better way to clean them," she grumbled as they filled the tenth tray. Dillon laughed.

"Some people do," he told her. "But dad's a bit old-fashioned about things like that."

At twelve o' clock precisely Vee Atkins called them to lunch. Tilly's mouth watered when she saw a large shepherd's pie steaming gently in the very center of the table, accompanied by chunks of homemade bread.

"Dig in," ordered Vee with a smile, plunging a spoon into the topping.

Fifteen minutes later Tilly sat back with her hands on her stomach wishing she had been a little less greedy.

"That was delicious!" she announced. Vee nodded, smiling broadly.

"Now, how has your first morning of work gone?" she asked. Tilly shrugged, glancing across at Dillon and he patted her enthusiastically on the back, making her feel suddenly sick.

"She did fine," he announced. "And Dad says we only have to do another hour this afternoon…"

"And then I can go and ride?" interrupted Tilly, eyes shining with anticipation even while her stomach churned at the thought of going into the woods again.

"And then you can ride," agreed Dillon. "But don't forget what you promised me yesterday…."

"Sunday, you said," she retorted.

"Sunday it is," he agreed.

Vee Atkins looked up at them, pink cheeked and smiling.

"What about Sunday?"

Dillon's response was immediate.

"Tilly is going to teach me to ride," he announced proudly.

Two hours later Tilly's thoughts were about as far removed as they could be from trays of newly washed brown eggs. Beneath her Sunny's broad back swayed as he trotted along the road toward Crickle Wood, and her fingers tightened on the reins. "What if, what if, what if?" she murmured, trying to push aside the terrifying memories that threatened to suffocate her. "What if nothing!" she announced out loud.

Sunny flicked his ears back in her direction and she leaned forward, patting his neck enthusiastically.

"You won't let me down this time, will you, boy?" she exclaimed. He blew through his nostrils, sidling out into the road, and as she gathered up her reins, clamping on her outside leg to keep him straight, the breath suddenly froze in her chest. For there just ahead of them, tall and imposing, was the Millennium gate… the gate between now… and then. Tilly gave a start and shook her head, bewildered. The gate between now and then? What was that supposed to mean? Where did these strange thoughts come from?

Feeling truly uneasy now, she took a long deep breath and vaulted from the saddle, her movements firm and precise, looping the reins through her arm before taking hold of the twisted metal bar. The gate swung open with a groan of resistance. Was it a sign? What if Sunny panicked again when she rode him through the trees?

"Don't be ridiculous," she told herself loudly. "You're just imagining things again. Come on, boy… let's go find Bess."

Way overhead the trees stretched majestically toward eternity. Tilly gazed up into their network of swaying branches, overcome by a sense of timelessness. Autumn leaves fell around her like golden rain; her heart beat overtime and her stomach churned. Where was the pathway with no gate? Where was Bess? Sunny's hooves echoed in the empty silence. A distant bird sang a solitary, single song, joining with the high-pitched moaning of the wind. Today... Tomorrow... Yesterday. All became fused into now, this moment in time... this moment of truth. There were those strange thoughts again! What was wrong with her today? "Get a grip on yourself," she muttered to herself, straightening in the saddle.

"Bess!"

Her voice floated up into the treetops and far, far away she thought she heard an answering cry.

"Bess!" she called again, urging Sunny forward, but when he leaped into canter her hands closed instantly on the reins as all her senses screamed in panic.

This time, to her relief, he responded instantly, as afraid as she of the unknown force that threatened. She ran her hand down his damp neck, absorbing the heat of him.

"Pull yourself together, Matilda," she said out loud, taking short, quick breaths. Beneath her Sunny stood completely still, poised for her command, as unsure as she but trusting his rider to take control.

"Come on," she told him with the slightest touch of her calves, and he walked forward eagerly, ears sharply pricked, nostrils flaring.

Where was Bess? Tilly had followed the main pathway right to its very end, past the clearing where an underground river gurgled to the surface momentarily before disappearing deep beneath the ground again. Sunny had plunged his nose into the rippling pool, drinking eagerly while she glanced nervously around. Where was the pathway with no gate?

She had called and called until her throat felt rasping and sore. It was so important to her that she found her friend and

60

she had expected it to be so easy; now it felt as of she had never even existed. She conjured up an image of Bess's smiling face, strong and so real. Of *course* she had existed… *but where was she*? A shiver rippled down her spine as she turned Sunny's head sadly toward home. The shadows were lengthening, making the woodland seem a dark and lonely place. Way above her head the wind whipped the treetops into a frenzy, and she pushed him into a brisk trot along the broad pathway. His hooves thudded on the thick bed of fallen leaves and her heart raced as memories came rushing back. Galloping hooves, the roar of traffic on the road ahead, the empty gap where the gate should have been.

"Bess!" she cried out one last time, and suddenly there she was, crossing the pathway just ahead astride her broad piebald cob. The image was so real. Bess, nut-brown, straight-backed, riding bareback and Domino, clean black and white shapes, flowing silver mane. And beyond them… Beyond them the pathway opened straight out into the road. Tilly froze, staring at the empty space where the gate should have been, unable to move, unable to think.

"Bess!" she screamed again but her voice just floated away, up into the treetops, mingling with the lonely cry of the wind. Bess was gone. The pathway stretched ahead of her like a tunnel through the trees, toward a patch of light in the distance… a patch of light against which the Millennium gate made an intricate pattern.

Her heart did a long, slow flip inside her chest and her stomach churned. What was happening to her? Had the whole world gone crazy or was it just inside her head? Panic wrapped itself around her with clinging fingers, leaving her weak and breathless as she urged Sunny forward toward the gate. Everything inside screamed at her to get away from this strange place and never come back, but still she glanced behind her, along the pathway. She had to find Bess, somehow, and if that meant

61

coming back here to face her fears, then she knew that that is what she would have to do. For deep inside, with total certainty, somehow she knew that her newfound friend needed her.

"Night or day," she whispered. "Night or day," came an answering cry. Or was it just the wind, moaning through the treetops?

Ahead of her the Millennium gate loomed, solid and familiar, and once again came the weird thoughts that made the breath freeze in her throat. *The gate between now and then.* That really was crazy.

"Come on, boy," she announced out loud as her hand closed around the cold, solid metal. "Let's go home."

Disappointment flooded over her as she rode back toward Cricklewood Farm. Normality settled around her again, but with it came a sense of failure. How could it be so difficult to find a pathway, and why hadn't Bess seen her? The image of the black and white horse and his dark haired rider flashed into her mind, solid and real. No way were they just a product of her imagination… and the gate…? She put that thought straight out of her head. Perhaps Bess was just in a rush to get somewhere. The Atkinses might know of her; she would ask them as soon as she got back, and next time she went to search the woods she would persuade Dillon to go with her.

Nerve ends still tingling no matter how hard she tried to be matter-of-fact about her experience, Tilly hurried Sunny along the lane. There was the old entrance to the farm; lopsided sign, overgrown track, chickens fluttering beneath the trees of the orchard. She dismounted to open the rickety gate and headed eagerly across the orchard, dragging Sunny behind her as she hurried over the rough ground. He hung back, grabbing for grass, and as she turned to reprimand him, her thoughts full of Bess, she saw Roger, the mottled gray rooster strutting toward her, accompanied by his clucking brood. He stopped and stared at her, beady eyes glaring from either side of his bright red comb, clucking angrily and flapping his wings. Tilly shrank back from his show of aggression and immediately realized her mistake, for he lowered his head, stretched out his neck and hurtled toward her, feathers fluffed out and sharp spurs stretching forward with every ungainly stride.

"Get away!" she screamed. "Get away!"

Sunny spooked and snorted, swinging around in the rooster's path. He leaped to the side and Tilly grabbed for the stirrup, hauling herself up to safety with a sigh of relief while Roger stood his ground, glaring up at her with an arrogant cry.

"Horrible bird," she told the strutting rooster as she turned Sunny up the hill toward the yard.

"That'll teach you not to use the back entrance," called Dillon as he opened the yard gate for her.

"You should be banned from keeping such a dangerous creature," she complained, smiling despite herself. He laughed out loud.

"You need to toughen up, girl. Anyway, see you tomorrow… Oh, and Dad says don't forget to shut the gate and make sure every thing is switched off before you leave."

Her face fell as helplessness clawed at her.

"You're going out?"

He nodded, already turning away.

"We're late already. We were waiting for you to come back. And don't forget what I told you…"

With that last remark he was gone, running off toward the front gate where his parents were waiting in the pickup truck. He squeezed in beside them, the vehicle rolled forward, and Tilly stood alone in the yard feeling suddenly very alone and vulnerable. She slipped down from the saddle and dragged the reins over Sunny's head.

"Come on," she urged wearily. "Let's get you fed."

✧ ✧ ✧ ✧ ✧

Darkness had already descended before Tilly set off for home. Her bicycle wobbled along the rutted lane, its headlamp making shaky patterns on the ground ahead. Had she remembered to fasten the gate? Had she... hadn't she? She imagined herself leaving the barn, sliding the bolt, saying goodbye to Sunny who totally ignored her. Fastening the gate... Yes, she had remembered... hadn't she? Her thoughts wandered, flitting back as always to Bess. If only she had been able to ask the Atkinses about her. Now it would have to wait until tomorrow. Impatience set in. What if Bess needed her now?

The sky, high above her, was velvety black, and on either side of the lane the trees made huge, dark, moving shapes. She shivered, clutching her handlebars. Suddenly all she wanted was the warmth and comfort of home, far away from woodland fires and pathways with invisible gates. Her legs pumped faster and her breath came in huge gasps as the last hill rose ahead of her. There were the lights of Millside cottage. There was her mother's car in the driveway. There was her mother on the step, eyes blazing, and lips tight with worry.

"I know," she cried, hurling her bicycle against the wall and leaning forward to get her breath, legs aching mercilessly. "I'm late."

"You know you aren't supposed to bike home in the dark," grumbled Fenna. "You should have called me..."

Tilly looked up at her, eyes dark with emotion and her mother stopped short.

"I think you'd better come inside and tell me all about it," she sighed.

"Well, someone must know this Bess girl," announced Fenna, after Tilly had relayed a detailed account of her entire day. "I mean, this is only a village, after all, so if she's local..."

64

They were sitting at the kitchen table clutching steaming mugs of hot chocolate while a frozen dinner defrosted in the microwave. It announced time up with a ping.

"Oh, she is," cried Tilly as her mother went across to turn the switch on to cook. "I know she is… Do you think I'm just overreacting?"

Fenna smiled and placed a sympathetic arm around her daughter's shoulders.

"Well, let's just say that you have always had a rather overactive imagination. I mean – don't get me wrong – I'm sure that there really was a fire and I know that you think she saved you, but are you sure that the gate hadn't just been left open? Try and think about it rationally, that's all."

"I suppose," agreed Tilly enthusiastically. She wanted to believe in rational; it made more sense and it was a whole lot less scary.

"Well, there you go," exclaimed Fenna sitting down again. She lifted her yellow flowered mug, drained the last drop of the sweet liquid and looked across at her daughter with a worried frown. "Now don't you dare go running off into the woods by yourself again. I'll ask around about Bess, and next time you go to search for her I'll come with you."

"Oh, Mom!" Tilly couldn't help but smile. "I know you want to help, but let's face it, you just don't have the time. Anyway, it looks as if I won't have much time to go searching for phantoms either, with all those eggs to wash."

Fenna McCloud put her head on one side and pursed her lips.

"Phantom, eh…? So you do think that you might have just imagined seeing this Bess person today. Are you sure that you didn't make up the whole thing?"

"No!" Tilly was adamant. "Of course not. I might have gotten a bit carried away about the gate vanishing and maybe the fire wasn't as bad as I thought, but Bess was real, and I know she wants to see me again."

"Well, don't you go searching for her by yourself," insisted Fenna.

Tilly's face softened. It was so good to have her mother back on her side again; she just hoped that it would last. Oh, if only her father would come back home…

The microwave pinged again and Fenna took two plates from the cupboard, deposited them on the side and turned toward Tilly with a smile.

"Come on then, sweetheart, make yourself useful and butter some bread. We'll eat in the living room."

It felt good, decided Tilly, to have talked everything over. Her mother's matter-of-fact approach had made her realize just how much her imagination had been running away with her. Of course the gate must simply have been left open and someone from around here was sure to know Bess. Tomorrow she would ask Bob and Vee.

She pulled the comforter tightly around her and lay in the semi darkness, watching the moon rise high in the sky through her window as she thought about her day. At least she had seen Bess again, even if it was only for a moment, and maybe tomorrow… She found herself suddenly looking forward to giving Dillon his lesson. There was just something about him that appealed to her… his teasing comments and that slow lopsided grin. She smiled to herself and closed her eyes, drifting into oblivion. Tomorrow everything would slide into place; she was sure of it.

chapter six

Sunny sidestepped, uneasy about the clumsy movements of his would-be rider. Tilly slapped him firmly on the shoulder.

"Stand," she ordered, before turning her attention to Dillon. "Now try not to dig your toe into him, and get more weight onto your right foot. The further you can get your weight underneath him the easier it will be to spring. It's just a knack."

"A darned difficult knack, if you ask me," grumbled Dillon, but his eyes were shining with excitement as he reached for the cantle of the saddle.

"I'll hold the stirrup," Tilly told him. "Now one… two… three."

With a broad grin Dillon sank lightly down into the saddle while Tilly kept a tight hold on the reins.

"Brilliant," she cried. "No… keep your legs still. Remember what I told you; if you go digging your heels into Sunny you'll be half way to Crickle Wood in five seconds."

The big dun gelding arched his neck, champing on the bit. Dillon touched him with his calves and he sprang forward.

"Now just go with him," ordered Tilly. "Let your hips swing and feel the movement beneath you. It's all about rhythm. And let your hands follow… Just hold the reins like I showed you and try to keep the same elastic contact with his mouth."

For ten minutes she kept tight hold of the rein as horse and rider walked around and around the yard, stopping and starting again and again until Dillon began to relax and find his balance.

"Right," announced Tilly. "Now I'm going to let go, so remember everything I told you and don't clamp your legs on."

She stood back cautiously at first, but, to her relief, Sunny tolerated Dillon's lack of experience with good grace. He reacted to each clumsy signal perfectly, and after only a little while she announced that they might try a trot.

When Dillon slipped to the ground fifteen minutes later his grin seemed to fill his whole face, making his irregular features appear for a moment almost handsome.

"That," he announced, "was fantastic."

Color flooded Tilly's cheeks. "I think you're a natural," she told him. "You'll be cantering before you know it."

"Well, there's no school this week, remember," he reminded her. "So can we have a lesson every day?"

"That," remarked Tilly, "depends on how much work your dad expects us to do.

Dillon grimaced. "Oh no, there's the long chicken shed to clean out. He was talking about it last night."

Tilly busied herself untacking Sunny and brushing him down. She still had to find time to look for Bess: no one was going to stop her from doing that.

"…And of course I *do* have to find time to ride myself…"

Her conscience prickled when Dillon's face fell.

"We'll find time for your lessons," she promised. "Don't worry, by the end of the week you'll be an expert."

"Dad says he'll buy another horse if I get on OK," he told her. "Then Mom can ride as well. She used to be really good."

Tilly's hand froze, brush held aloft. "What sort of horse did she used to have?" she asked uneasily.

"Well, it was before I was born of course, but I've seen some pictures. One was an old hunter that she used to show jump before she met my dad and the other was an Arab…"

Suddenly Tilly couldn't breathe. She walked out into the autumn sunshine on wooden legs with a roaring sound in her head and Bess's voice in her ears.

They have two horses of their own, an old hunter and an Arab. I've seen them in the field beside the road.

Her head was spinning. How had Bess known that? It must be some sort of coincidence; perhaps the two horses she saw didn't belong to the Atkinses at all.

"Are you OK?" Dillon's face hovered in front of her and reality rushed back. She nodded vaguely, trying to smile.

"Sorry, I just feel a bit dizzy, that's all."

He ushered her toward the wall and insisted she sit down. "Is that any better?"

Touched by his concern, Tilly's fears faded just a little.

What are you afraid of anyway? she asked herself. The answer came at once. *The unknown and the unexplainable.* There was one person who *could* explain it, though, and she was determined to find her.

"When did you say your parents would be back?" she asked.

Dillon sat down beside her with a worried expression on his usually affable features.

"Just after lunch. Why… are you feeling worse?"

"No," she insisted, standing up. She shook her hair out into a golden cloud around her face and then twisted it all back up into a ponytail.

"You have lovely hair."

He blurted out the compliment, grimacing as if surprised at his own words. Tilly saw the discomfort in his face and smiled.

"Thank you," she said, meaning it. For the briefest moment she held his gaze and suddenly her fear faded, replaced by a sense of determination. The truth, that's all she wanted, surely someone must know who Bess was. She must try not to let her imagination run away with her.

"I need to ask them about the girl I met in the woods that day," she explained. "You know, Bess."

Dillon nodded. "The one who you said saved you when Sunny bolted."

See? she thought to herself, irritation prickling, *even he doesn't really believe me.*

Vee Atkins had left them a huge lunch of cheese and cold meats and pie. Tilly became aware of them now, heavy in the base of her stomach.

"She did save me," she insisted. "And I need to find her. Surely your parents must know most people around here."

Dillon shrugged. "Well you can ask them yourself," he told her, pointing toward the lane.

As soon as the pickup truck shuddered to a halt Tilly was at the passenger side door. Vee clambered out and handed her a large plastic bag to carry.

"Might as well make yourselves useful now that you're here," she said, lifting two more from behind the seat and handing them to Dillon. "Come on, let's get the kettle on, I'm dying for a cup of tea."

"No tea for these two if they haven't finished that shed," grumbled her husband.

Dillon laughed. "Well, you can stop moaning, because we finished it before lunch, and…" He stopped, smiling broadly. "I've had my first riding lesson."

His mother's face lit up.

"And how did you do?"

"He did well," Tilly announced. "I think he's a natural, and Sunny behaved really well, which helped."

It wasn't until the tea was brewed and they were chewing thick slices of freshly baked bread, that Tilly found her moment.

"Do either of you know a girl called Bess?" she asked, her

71

heart pounding. "She is about fifteen and kind of sturdily built. She rides a piebald cob."

Bob Atkins frowned, shaking his head slowly from side to side.

"Bess…Bess. There was a Bess once. Do you remember her, Vee? The girl who used to ride along the lane."

A concentrated frowned appeared on his wife's smooth plump face, and then she raised her eyebrows and laughed.

"Don't take any notice of him," she said, looking at Tilly. "I know who he means, but it must be twenty years since *she* came riding by. What happened to her, anyway?"

Memory dawned even before Bob could answer the question. Her face fell; echoing the deep sadness in her husband's eyes, and in the moment before she started to speak Tilly felt a heavy weight settle itself in her heart.

"It was terrible..."

She looked directly at Tilly, outrage expelling the sadness.

"… for such a young girl to die like that."

"Like what?"

She shook her head. "Oh, you don't want to bother yourself with bygone tragedies. I don't know why Bob mentioned her in the first place."

"It was the name Bess. It just reminded me, that's all," cut in her husband. "And she rode a piebald cob, didn't she?"

"Yes," Vee sighed, looking at Tilly. "We didn't know her that well, to be honest, as we hadn't lived here long, but I remember she used to wave as she trotted by."

"Tell me what happened…"

Tilly's eyes pleaded. Suddenly it seemed very important to hear the story of this other Bess from long ago. After all she may be a relative of *her* Bess… Or maybe…? It didn't bear thinking about.

"It was in all the papers," went on Vee. "What was her last name, Bob?"

Her husband shrugged. "All I can remember is Bess."

Vee took a sip of her tea and swallowed, holding the warm cup between her hands as she tried to collect her thoughts.

"No," she eventually exclaimed. "I know that the local paper called her Elizabeth, but I can't for the life of me remember her last name. We just knew her as Bess."

"What happened to her?" Tilly's voice rang out.

All eyes turned toward her, and Vee glanced across at her husband as if for approval before placing her cup carefully down onto the saucer. Tilly found herself staring at it, vivid red poppies against a stark white background. She was shaking somewhere deep down inside herself, unsure of *why* this meant so much, just knowing that it did.

"There was a fire," began Vee in a hushed tone. "She was trying to save her horse and the roof collapsed…"

"What…! They both died?"

Tilly felt as if she was choking, as if the smoke from that long gone fire was suffocating her too. An image of Bess's face flashed into her mind, nut brown and smiling. But it wasn't *her* Bess who had died, was it? It couldn't be. A relative, it *must* have been a relative.

"Don't look so worried, hon," remarked Bob with a broad grin. "It was a terrible thing, but it all happened years ago, long before you were even born."

"Where did she live?"

Tilly tried to compose herself, forcing the vivid images out of her head. It was Vee who answered.

"She and her father had a cottage right in the center of Crickle Wood. He was a funny fellow; brought the girl up all on his own after her mother died when she was just a toddler. He wasn't there on the night of the fire, which made it even worse. The poor girl was all alone, and they say that if she hadn't tried to save her horse she would have been fine."

Tilly felt a rushing sound inside her head; images jumbled

together, each one fighting for her attention. Fire and smoke and screams… Oh, the screams. She placed her hands over her face but the images went on and on…

"Are you all right, hon?"

Comforting hands on her shoulders brought reality back, and with it confusion.

"I knew we shouldn't have told her," grumbled Bob.

"No!" Tilly was adamant. "I wanted to know."

She took a breath and forced a smile onto her face. "As you said, it all happened ages ago. It's just…"

She looked down at her hands.

"Just what?"

Vee's voice was soft in her ears.

"Just… so sad."

For a moment there was silence as their thoughts all turned to that moment in the night, when a lonely young girl had cried out her fear in the darkness and died trying to save her dearest friend.

It was Bob who moved first.

"Come on," he ordered gruffly. "No point making yourselves miserable over something that happened well over twenty years ago. We have work to do."

"Work… work… work," grumbled Dillon, standing up. "Come on, Matilda McCloud, you promised me another lesson later, remember."

"You can leave that until we've caught Roger and trimmed his dratted spurs," insisted Bob. "He ripped my boot yesterday. The only person he seems to like nowadays is your mother."

"Maybe we should think about getting rid of him," suggested Dillon. His idea met with a look of disgust from his father.

"Get rid of Roger!" he exclaimed. "Why, he's just as much a part of the place as you or me. Anyway, once we've clipped his spurs he'll be no bother at all, and I thought I

74

might repair the fence around the old orchard. Then he won't be able to come up into the yard and frighten the life out of the mailman."

"Does he?" giggled Tilly. "Does he really go for the mailman?"

"He didn't dare deliver the mail yesterday," Dillon told her, and suddenly the two of them were laughing hysterically.

"Crazy kids," remarked Bob, pulling on his coat. "Come on, I'll find you something to laugh at."

The capture of the mottled gray rooster proved to be far easier than Tilly had imagined. Bob Atkins simply grabbed him from behind, gripping his hands hard around the powerful bird's wings while Dillon deftly removed the offending spurs with a pair of clippers.

"There," he announced, releasing the affronted rooster. Roger stared at him with beady yellow eyes, ruffling his feathers and squawking his disgust to the entire neighborhood.

"That was neatly done," remarked Tilly. "Maybe you should think about becoming a vet…"

Dillon froze, appearing to concentrate all his attention on the angry bird.

"Don't *you* think he'd make a good vet?" she went on, turning toward Bob. He shrugged and picked up the clippers from where Dillon had dropped them, placing them carefully back into his toolbox.

"Not a bad idea, I suppose. It's always good to have a profession. What do you think, son?"

Dillon seemed suddenly to burst into life. He looked up at his father, his face a dull red.

"It would be great, but… I mean. Well, I'm going to work here, aren't I?"

Bob laughed out loud.

"What! So you think that I'm ready for the scrap heap already, do you? Anyway, think of how much money I'd save on vet's bills."

The three of them fell into step as they headed back across to the yard, Dillon deep in thought while Bob whistled in a low key. Tilly was determined to push her advantage home.

"So how about it?" she asked, nudging Dillon firmly in the ribs. He jumped sideways, knocking against his father who smiled and nodded.

"You should think about it," he suggested, heading for the house.

"I'll do that," agreed Dillon happily.

"I'll go and tack up for your lesson," offered Tilly with a broad grin. Dillon took hold of her shoulders, turning her to face him.

"Thanks for that."

"No problem," she insisted. "I've always wanted a big brother, and now it feels like I've got one."

Disappointment flickered in his blue eyes as he watched her walk off in the direction of the barn, and he exhaled deeply before following his father toward the back door.

As Tilly heaved her saddle over the door and set to work with a body brush and currycomb, her thoughts drifted back toward Bess, the Bess who had died trying to save her horse. Would she do that for Sunny? Oh, she hoped so, but would she have the courage? She thought about her Bess. She would have the courage, no question about that. The girl who died had to be related to her, she just had to be; there were too many comparisons.

As she eased the buckle into the girth tab Dillon appeared in the doorway. She glanced across at him before running her fingers beneath the leather girth to smooth down the hair.

"I have a deal for you," she announced.

He frowned cautiously.

"What kind of deal?"

"I'll give you a lesson and then you can…"

She let the saddle flap settle back into place and looked him straight in the eye.

"…Come with me to look for Bess's house."

"What!"

He stared at her with dawning horror.

"You must be joking! I've heard that story about the girl who was killed in the fire; they say that the cottage hasn't been touched since the day she died. It's so overgrown that you can hardly find it, and anyway…"

He stopped short and looked away.

"Anyway what?" cried Tilly.

The idea to find the cottage was so firmly embedded in her mind that she knew she would do it, with or without Dillon's help. The thought of going there alone, however, brought a sick feeling to the base of her stomach.

"What?" she repeated.

"Some people say that it's haunted…"

There, it was out. He looked at Tilly, gauging her reaction, and for a moment she froze, trying to control the pounding of her heart.

"I don't believe in ghosts," she announced, forcing a confident note into her voice. "Don't tell me you're afraid!"

"Of course not," announced Dillon, but as he opened the barn door and motioned her to lead Sunny outside she saw that his face was deathly white.

"You are!" she exclaimed. "You're afraid of ghosts."

"I am not," he insisted.

She stood up very tall, elation pulsating through every vein.

"Prove it then. Prove that you're not scared by coming with me tomorrow."

He stared at her for a moment, then he exhaled and his whole body seemed to deflate.

"You're on," he told her. "Give me another lesson now and I'll come with you just as soon as we can get away tomorrow."

It had seemed such a good idea in the bright light of day, thought Tilly, to go and find this long ago Bess's cottage; as if she was doing something positive to try and find *her* Bess. As she rode home through the twilight, however, it suddenly seemed like a foolhardy plan. What if the cottage really was haunted? You did hear about things like that… why, only last week she had seen a TV program about a haunted church. Her fingers gripped more tightly around the handlebars and she increased her pace, legs aching as they pounded around and around.

"You have to do it… You have to do it… You have to do it," she repeated again and again in time with her pumping knees.

To her disappointment her mother wasn't home. Would she have told her what she was planning to do if she had been there, wondered Tilly? The answer came back at once. No…! No, she wouldn't tell *anyone* where she and Dillon were going tomorrow.

She put her bike away, unlocked the back door and burst into the warm comfort of the kitchen. On the very center of the kitchen table was a heaped plate, carefully covered in plastic wrap, and a large, quickly scrawled note.

I will be back at eight. Give this five minutes on full power. Love, Mom.

The fire in the living room stove was still glowing and she threw on another log, watching the yellow flames curl hungrily around it before going back into the kitchen to warm up her meal, stomach rumbling. It seemed ages since those cookies at snack time. She picked up the plate and pulled off the plastic wrap.

Chicken! Images of Roger and all Tilly's other clucking

charges sprang into her mind. Could she really eat chicken? She took it across to the trashcan, knife suspended. Roasted potatoes, crisply brown, and two large slices of enticing white meat, floating in a rich gravy. The tantalizing aroma drifted up her nostrils and she breathed in deeply, mouth watering.

"Sorry, Roger," she silently apologized, sliding the plate into the microwave and switching it on.

Fifteen minutes later, stomach full and eyelids heavy, she sat on the sofa in front of the TV. Crickle Wood and the hidden cottage seemed a whole lot less scary in the warmth and comfort of home; suddenly it seemed like a fun idea to go there with Dillon tomorrow. She felt her nerves beginning to evaporate, leaving a vague sense of euphoria. Yes, a bit of fun, that's all it would be. Ghosts! As if! She didn't even believe in them.

The images on the screen blurred and Tilly looked up, confused. She could hear her mother's voice in the kitchen. What time was it? Bleary eyed, she focused on her watch. Could it really be nine o'clock already?

"Did you enjoy your dinner?"

Fenna McCloud's face materialized around the living room door.

"Sorry I'm late. I had a meeting that went on and on… would you like a drink?"

"Hot chocolate would be nice," responded Tilly with a sleepy smile. "And then I'm going to bed."

When the telephone on the window ledge began to ring she determinedly ignored it; perhaps her mother would pick it up in the kitchen.

"Could you answer that please, honey?" called Fenna. Tilly sighed and stood up, stretching her arms into the air as she walked across toward the jarring sound.

"Where's your mother?"

Her father's voice on the other end of the line was loud and angry, distant and alien. Her heart clamped tight shut.

"Dad, is that you?" she whispered.

"Sorry, hon." His voice softened. "I didn't mean to shout. I've got some things to straighten out with your mother, that's all."

"When are you coming home?"

He ignored her question, answering it with another.

"Where is she, your mother? I'm in a rush here and this is costing a fortune."

Tilly felt tears brim up at the back of her eyes. What had happened to the dad she used to spend so much time with, the one who had gone with her to buy the young, scrawny Sunny?

"Sunny's doing fine," she blurted out. "We've changed stables."

"That's good, honey."

His voice was polite and disinterested, a stranger's voice. The tears seemed to fill her whole head.

"I'll take it." Her mother's impatient voice cut in on the line from the kitchen phone.

"Bye, Dad," whispered Tilly, placing the receiver down with a thump as her mother began to shout.

For a moment she stood and listened to the angry sounds issuing from the kitchen, unaware of the sense of them. Pictures sprang into her mind; her father laughing, holding her mother in his arms, smiling down at her with pride in his gray eyes… caring.

She stifled a sob and placed her hands over her ears, misery building behind the dam she had so carefully constructed the night he went away. As it began to crumble she raced out of the room and ran up the stairs to throw herself down onto her bed. If only she could talk to Bess – she would understand, she would know what to do.

"You OK, honey?"

Her mother's voice from the doorway was soft and gentle,

caring. Oh, why couldn't she get along with him? Why couldn't she persuade him to come home?

"Your dad didn't mean to be short with you. It's me he's angry with. He said to say sorry and he'll call you tomorrow."

Tilly turned her face into the pillow.

"He shouldn't bother."

She felt her mother's hand on her shoulder and shrugged it away, turning to look up at her.

"He's never coming back, is he?" she cried.

"Oh, Tilly," Fenna McCloud's face contorted. "It's just you and me now, I'm afraid."

She stood up slowly and walked out of the room. Tilly listened to the thud of her feet on the stairs before sitting up and rubbing her eyes.

Your mother must be so angry and confused.

There was Bess's voice in her ears again, all knowing. Tomorrow… tomorrow she would find her.

Her mother was sitting in the chair beside the fire, crumpled and crying.

"It's OK, Mom."

Tilly felt like she was the parent and her mother the child.

"We've still got each other," she said softly. "Come on, I'll make that hot chocolate."

The dam was back, firm and strong, keeping emotion at bay while her mind thought about tomorrow and what she would say to Bess if she found her. But Dillon would be there. Maybe she should go alone. The answer came at once, screaming out at her. No! No way would she go to search for the cottage on her own. A shiver rippled down her spine as she thought of that other, long ago Bess, fighting to save her horse and dying alone in the woods. Would she do that for Sunny? An image of his lovely head flashed into her mind, amber eyes soft and gentle, silky coat warm beneath her touch. She hoped so – oh, how she hoped so.

81

chapter seven

Everything seemed to come back to the dratted Millennium gate, thought Tilly, as its imposing, ornate structure came into view. It felt like the gate between two different worlds. She shivered, pushing her fancies firmly aside. Her mother was always telling her not to be so over imaginative.

"Good looking gate, isn't it?" remarked Dillon. He had been biking along in silence for a while, just up ahead of her, and now he turned to look back, his face shadowed by the trees. Tilly smiled broadly in his general direction. Was that tension she could hear in his voice; was he secretly just as nervous as she?

"It's certainly different," she agreed. "I suppose you must know your way around these woods really well."

Dillon stood up on his pedals, slowing his bicycle right down for Sunny to catch up.

"I used to play here sometimes when I was a kid, but if you're asking if I've ever been to this cottage of yours before, well, I haven't."

"It's not *my* cottage, its Bess's," retorted Tilly. "And surely you must have been at least tempted to look for it."

He shook his head, blue eyes twinkling mischievously. "You must be joking... not after all the stories I've heard."

Sunny pranced and sidled as her fingers tightened on the reins.

"You're just trying to rattle me," she exclaimed.

"But are you sure of that?"

Dillon jumped off his bicycle and looked up at her, one hand shading his eyes from the bright autumn sunlight, hiding his expression. Sunny snorted, sensing his rider's unease, and she took a deep breath, stroking his neck with short quick strokes.

"Of course I'm sure," she retorted. "I don't believe in ghosts and I don't think that there can be anything even remotely frightening about a derelict cottage. Anyway, it's probably fallen down altogether by now."

"Who are you trying to convince?" asked Dillon. "Me… or yourself?"

For a moment a shadow blocked out the sunshine and she caught a glimpse of the mischief in his eyes.

A giggle bubbled up her throat. "Myself, probably," she admitted.

He laughed, shaking his head as he moved across to open the gate. It groaned on its hinges, complaining at his touch, and she felt something tighten inside her.

"OK, then."

Taking charge, Dillon ushered them through.

"Come on… the sooner we get there the sooner we can go home again."

Behind them the gate clanged shut with the echo of finality, and ahead… Tilly shivered as she turned Sunny onto the pathway… What *was* ahead of them?

"Now where should we start?" asked Dillon. He had left his bike hidden in the bushes beside the gate, and now he walked right next to Sunny's shoulder, keeping close.

"Right in the very center, I suppose," suggested Tilly. "Near the clearing where that stream gurgles up and then disappears again."

He glanced up at her, smiling.

"And now we have disappearing streams?"

"No…!" she exclaimed. "I mean, it's an underground

83

stream, and it surfaces just in one kind of pool right in the center of the clearing. Oh, you must have seen it, you're just teasing me again."

They progressed in silence then for a while. She could feel his shoulder pressing against her leg as the track narrowed, lending comfort from the nerves that jangled inside her head as she glanced uneasily from side to side, searching for a glimpse of an overgrown wall, a roof collapsed with time, or even any sign of fire at all. Surely there should be some sign of the fire that had started all this. Even if the whole cottage had been burned to the ground there would still be something left.

Way up above their heads skeletal branches swayed as a sudden wind threw moving shadows onto the pathway beneath their feet. Sunny snorted, sidling into the trees, hooves slipping on a thick lair of soft damp leaves as Tilly tried to steady him.

"Come on," yelled Dillon, reaching for Sunny's reins, but the powerful gelding tossed his head, plunging further into the woodland.

Tilly's senses seemed suddenly heightened as she struggled for control. The aroma of the forest filled her nostrils, damp leaves brushed her face and all around her the trees closed in… so many shades of green. And then came lights, flickering and flashing, golden and yellow in the murky darkness. Sunny froze, standing totally motionless for one full second and in that second, as fear clamped down on Tilly's senses, Dillon took a firm hold of his rein, drawing him back to the safety of the pathway.

She gasped and took a breath, eyes searching frantically for the flickering flames. The air was rich with the aroma of damp wood and moss, clean and sweet with no acrid scent of smoke to mar it. Tears welled up behind her eyes as relief flooded in. Sunlight, that's all it was… sunlight flickering through the moving branches.

"Look, Tilly, should we just forget it for today?"

Dillon's voice was low and urgent; his eyes dark with emotion as he held firmly on to Sunny's rein.

Her response was instantaneous.

"No! I'll be fine now, honest."

"You don't look fine."

She glanced around nervously, drawing confidence from the peacefulness of their surroundings. The wind had dropped as suddenly as it started and the trees seemed strangely still.

"It's just me being stupid and pathetic," she admitted. "For a moment I thought that the sunlight flickering through the trees was flames again, like last time. It spooked me, that's all."

"Yes, but it frightened Sunny as well, that's what worries me," declared Dillon. "And let's face it, maybe it was just those flickering lights that spooked him the last time. There isn't actually any sign of the fire you thought you saw then, is there? So what if he bolts with you again?"

Suddenly Tilly felt very strong.

"He won't," she insisted. "You have to believe me, there really was a fire. I know we haven't seen any signs of it… but… well… we must just be in the wrong part of the woods, that's all. It was my *own* panic that spooked Sunny this time, not the wind or the lights. He trusts me, you see, and I let him down."

"But what if I'm right… and what if…"

She met the doubt in Dillon's eyes with a confident smile.

"What if I spook him again…" she finished. "Well, you're not and I won't. Don't ask me why, I just suddenly feel really strong. I know I've been totally overreacting… Look…" She cast her hand around the expanse of woodland that surrounded them. What is there to spook me, anyway? There's hardly going to be a fire again, is there? Everything's wet."

Dillon smiled ruefully.

"I never thought of that."

"And let's face it, what are we looking *for*? A derelict cottage… Not much harm in that either, is there?"

"Not unless you believe in ghosts," he remarked, gauging her reaction.

"Well, I certainly don't," she insisted too loudly. "Now come on, we're almost at the clearing. The cottage must be around here somewhere. I'll tie Sunny to that tree over there and we'll have a proper look around."

The big dun gelding gazed at her with soulful amber eyes as she unfastened the lead rope from around his neck and secured it firmly to a stout sapling. She rubbed the crest of his neck, encouraging him to pick at the grass.

"It's OK, boy, I'm not going far," she murmured. He blew softly through his nostrils, showering her with droplets, and she laughed, slapping him affectionately on the shoulder.

Dillon, however, watched with concern.

"You're sure that he can't get loose?"

She double-checked the head collar he wore beneath his bridle and then the slipknot she had tied, making sure that the end was through the loop.

"No," she remarked, with one last look. "I think he'll be fine. As long as we're not gone too long."

"Come on, then," he urged and side-by-side they left the serenity of the clearing and headed into the trees.

Excitement pushed aside all other emotions as they plunged into the undergrowth, eagerly looking for crumbling stonework or traces of a long gone pathway. They searched in silence, keeping in sight of each other but concentrating totally on their task.

"There," screamed Tilly at last. "Over there!"

Through the trees she could see something square and bulky; a wall, could it be the remnants of a wall?

Dillon rushed to join her, adrenalin pumping as together

they fought their way toward their goal. Briars tore at their legs and scratched their hands as they pushed their way through, clawing at them, as if to try and protect the place that had remained untouched for twenty years.

"Look!" cried Tilly, dragging ivy from the barrier ahead of her. "It's a gate, I'm sure it's a gate."

The creeping tendrils resisted her efforts, clinging tightly to the wooden bars with twenty years of growth. Dillon joined in, as eager as she, and gradually the shape of the gate was revealed and on it, right in the center of the very top bar, green with years of neglect, was an oval sign. Tilly spat on her sleeve and began frantically rubbing at the flaking paint.

"Careful," advised Dillon. "You'll rub the name off altogether if you do that… Here."

He pulled a bandana from his pocket and followed Tilly's example, spitting hard into the middle of it before beginning to work carefully on the decaying sign.

Tilly watched, mesmerized, unaware that she was holding her breath until she began to feel faint. She gasped, hand on heart, excitement clawing at her as the words on the sign were slowly revealed.

"Ivy Cottage," she cried. "This must be it… this must be the entrance to Bess's house."

"I wish you'd stop presuming that the Elizabeth who died in this cottage all those years ago has something to do with that Bess girl you met in the woods," groaned Dillon.

Tilly glared at him.

"Well, it seems pretty obvious to me. I mean, Bess *is* short for Elizabeth after all, so that's a bit of a coincidence, and I'm sure that she told me that she lived in Crickle Wood."

Dillon rolled his eyes in exasperation.

"Did she actually tell you that?"

Tilly looked at the ground, her excitement evaporating.

"Well… no… but she did say that she lived near here."

Dillon was still not convinced.

"How near? Did she actually tell you how near?"

"Well…"

Tilly screwed up her face, trying to remember.

"She just kind of waved her arm and said she lived with her dad, over that way," she admitted, pointing in the general direction of the woodland behind them.

"Well, Burnbrook village is just over there," exclaimed Dillon. "So she might live right in the very center of it, for all you know, and anyway, I can't understand why I've never seen her. She probably doesn't live around here at all."

"I'm sure she does," insisted Tilly unconvincingly.

Dillon smiled. "Look," he began in a kindly tone. "I am quite happy to look for this Elizabeth girl's cottage with you. To be honest it's scary to think that she actually died, here in this very wood, all those years ago – especially in such a horrible way – but you have to stop believing that she's an ancestor of this Bess girl you're so obsessed with."

Tilly lifted her chin and looked him straight in the eye.

"I am *not* obsessed with her. She went out of her way to help me and I owe her, that's all. She's a friend."

Dillon sighed, stuffed his filthy bandana back into his pocket, and started to climb the rotting gate. When the top rail cracked beneath his weight Tilly laughed out loud.

"OK," she agreed, lifting her hand. "Truce."

He jumped down onto the other side of the gate and leaned across it to slap her palm.

"Truce," he agreed. "Now let's find this cottage you're so interested in."

It seemed to Tilly, as they grew closer to what surely must have been Elizabeth's cottage, that the day grew suddenly

89

darker. She clasped her arms about herself, glancing around nervously. Dillon had no such reservations.

"Come on," he cried, pushing aside the overhanging branches. "Don't tell me you're scared. It happened twenty years ago you know. There's probably nothing left anyway."

She followed dubiously, her heart beating a tattoo against her rib cage however hard she tried to convince herself that there was nothing to be afraid of. Deep, deep down inside herself, she still nurtured the feeling that this place had something to do with Bess... but what? Perhaps Dillon was right after all. Perhaps Bess had nothing to do with Elizabeth at all, and perhaps the fire in the woods that day really *had* all been in her imagination. For a moment she hesitated, overcome by such confusion that her legs seemed to turn to jelly.

"Come on!" he yelled again, and she forced herself to move... toward the dark shapes she could see now through the trees. They were walls, she realized, quickening her pace... the walls of an enclosure, broken down and totally taken over by nature. Had someone really lived here once? She tried to imagine the place as it must have been then; neat stone walls enclosing the cottage that lay just ahead, Elizabeth's cottage. Twenty years ago it had been a home, and now it was merely a black, overgrown hulk amongst the trees.

A sudden breeze sprang up, whistling through the treetops, cutting into her like a knife. She shuddered and started to run, eager to catch up to Dillon who was already entering the crumbling, burned-out ruin.

The first thing Tilly noticed, as she walked through what had obviously once been an entrance, was the silence. Not even a bird fluttered through the branches that hung down over the broken-down walls. A deep sadness settled around her in a heavy cloud as she thought about that poor long-ago girl, fighting to save her horse from the all-consuming flames. She closed her eyes, suddenly wanting to be anywhere but here, where the melancholy threatened to suffocate her.

"Look," cried Dillon, his voice high-pitched with excitement. "This must have been the living room."

He disappeared through another doorway, diving into the heart of the cottage with no thought in his head for the feelings she was going through. Didn't he care about Elizabeth?

With a sense of shock she saw chairs and a table, ordinary things, black with age and almost taken over now by nature itself, but still there to prove that someone had once lived here... loved here… *died here*! She cowered back against the wall, her hand on her heart, wanting to call out to Dillon, to beg him to leave this place undisturbed, but when she opened her mouth no sound came out. She stood motionless, her eyes moving involuntarily around the room. A blackberry bush had squeezed itself over the couch that stood beneath the glassless window, its prickly tendrils wrapped around the shaped wooden legs. And beside it a cabinet leaned over precariously, pushed aside by a sapling oak. Dillon moved toward it, pulling at the handles. The doors swung open with surprising ease, as if eager to give up its secrets, and he let out a cry of excitement.

"Look at this!"

He held out a box, black and mildewed, but still recognizable as a jigsaw puzzle. Gently he wiped away the dirt and, amazingly, the picture on the lid was gradually revealed.

"Why… Tilly!" he exclaimed, beckoning her over. "This could be a picture of you and Sunny.

Hardly daring to look, but unable not to, Tilly took in the faded picture of the puzzle that nestled in its box as good as new. Sunny looked out at her with huge, soft eyes and beside him… She shivered… beside him; arm draped casually over the arched crest of his muscular neck… was a tall, slim girl with long, fair hair and a wide smile.

"See," cried Dillon with delight. "It is, isn't it? It's you and Sunny. That seriously is the weirdest thing I have ever seen. I'm taking it home, and when I've finished it I'm going to put it in a frame."

Tilly's response was immediate. Everything inside her recoiled from his suggestion with such violence that she began to physically shake.

"Hey."

Dillon's eyes grew wide with alarm and he placed a reassuring hand on her arm.

"Take a breath," he advised. "You're getting carried away. Look…"

He swept his hand around the small, sad space, forcing her to take in her surroundings.

"No one has been here for twenty years, and that's what's making you feel weird. These things have just been left to rot. No one wants them. After the girl died in the fire they say that her father just walked away and left everything behind. No one knew if he was coming back, so everything was left just as it was. I don't think that he'll be coming back now, though… do you?"

Tilly shook her head.

"So I may as well at least make this poor jigsaw of you."

"It's not me!" cried Tilly. "It's just a girl and a horse."

"All right then," he laughed. "Then I'll make this jigsaw of the girl and horse who *look* just like you and Sunny. Perhaps poor Elizabeth will appreciate it finally being done."

He walked away then, intent upon exploring the rest of the buildings, but Tilly hung back. She didn't want to see the place where Elizabeth had fought so hard to save her horse… and failed in the attempt.

When she eventually went out into what had once been a small yard, her eyes were immediately drawn to the blackened, crumbling pile of stones facing her. The cobblestones beneath her feet were almost totally overgrown with weeds, saplings forced their way through tiny crevices in the broken walls, and a silver birch tree thrust its branches through the space where a window used to be. It seemed that the building had become a part of the woodland, totally taken over by nature herself, with no sign left of the terrible tragedy that had once occurred there. But Tilly knew. With no shadow of doubt in her mind she knew. This was the place.

She shuddered, clasping her arms about herself.

"Come on," she yelled to Dillon, who was rooting about amongst the rubble. "Let's get out of here."

He looked around at her with a grin, totally unaffected by the emotion that threatened to suffocate her, until he saw the expression on her face.

His jaw dropped instantly. "Do you think that this is…?"

"I know it is," she answered simply.

For a moment they both stood motionless, unable to take in the awesome truth. Could a young girl really have died in this very place?

"How do you know?"

The color drained from Dillon's face as he whispered the question.

"You can see…"

Tilly's response was immediate but the words stuck in her throat and she shook her head, pointing to where a burned and blackened timber hung across what had once been a doorway. Signs of fire seemed to be suddenly everywhere. Jarred wood, stones blackened by the flames that had once consumed this place…. Once consumed Elizabeth and the horse she died for.

A heavy knot settled in her chest. It had been a black and white cob… just like Domino. A vivid image of the scene flooded her imagination and she pushed it aside as an ocean of tears forced her face into her hands.

Dillon's hand settled on her shoulder.

"It was all a very long time ago," he murmured. "Come on… Let's go home."

She allowed herself to be led away, but the stifling sadness made her movements stiff and awkward. It was as if her legs no longer seemed to function properly, and the pain in her heart seemed to swell with every stride.

Neither of them spoke again until they reached the place where Sunny had been tied and found him gone. The broken rope swung from the tree where Tilly had so carefully fastened it and the churned up ground around the base of the trunk showed how agitated the big dun gelding must have become. Burning stables and long ago tragedies faded instantly as she looked at Dillon in panic.

"Now calm down," he insisted. "He can't have gone far, and he can't get out of the woods anyway, so we're sure to find him."

"Can't he? But what about the pathway with no gate?"

Dillon looked straight at her, his blue eyes clear and honest.

"There is no pathway with no gate," he told her simply.

Tilly had no time to absorb the enormity of his information. Relief flooded in and she scoured the ground for telltale tracks.

"Come on," she yelled, running off into the trees.

They heard his hoofbeats before they saw him, thumping rhythmically along a leaf-strewn track.

"Sunny!" called Tilly. "Come on, boy," and suddenly there he was, head up and nostrils flaring. Her heart thumped loudly in her chest and she stood, feet splayed, as he approached, re-membering how Bess had stopped him in mid-gallop.

This time, however, he slowed to a walk as soon as he saw them, nickering furiously, nose extended and head lowered with relief.

"That'll teach you to break loose," Dillon told him. Tilly

94

just grabbed the fraying end of the broken lead rope, flung her arms around his solid neck and looked up at Dillon through a blur of tears.

"Let's go home," she pleaded.

"Best suggestion you've made all day," he agreed, tucking the jigsaw under his arm.

"I'd forgotten about that," remarked Tilly, as they set off side-by-side along the pathway. "Are you really going to make it?"

He nodded determinedly, lifting it up to look at the faded picture.

"Of course I am. It lasted so well in that cupboard for twenty years that the least I can do is actually make it. I told you, I'm going to frame it; it'll remind me of you and Sunny."

"I think Elizabeth would like that," sighed Tilly. "And I think you're right, it does look a bit like us. Weird, isn't it?"

"This…" announced Dillon with a grin, "if you haven't already noticed, has been a seriously weird kind of day."

chapter eight

The yellow glow of electric light gave Sunny's coat an extra gleam as he stood, knee deep in straw, ears flicked eagerly toward his mistress. He nickered, long and low, tossing his head impatiently in anticipation of his feed.

"It's coming in a minute," she told him firmly, standing back to absorb the effects of her hard work. Her shoulders ached satisfyingly, physical effort briefly dispelling the tension and heartache of the day. She wrapped her arms around herself, temporarily fighting off the memories that would later come to haunt her. The scorched shape on Sunny's flank was almost gone now, just a faint mark in his rapidly thickening coat, reminding her of the fire. She reached out to touch it, tracing her fingers over the roughness of it, turning sharply away as emotion swelled inside her. However much she refused to admit her doubts to Dillon, deep down inside fear and confusion seemed sometimes to take over her whole being. Why had they been unable to find any signs of the fire that was so real to her? Was she really going crazy? Maybe Dillon was right about it all being inside her head. The thought was too scary to contemplate.

Her eyes fastened once again onto the dark mark on Sunny's flank. There *had* been a fire, though, for here was the proof right in front of her. Confidence flowed back. Sometimes she felt as if she was being buffeted this way and that by events beyond her control. With a determined sigh she stood up tall and squared her shoulders, patting Sunny firmly on the shoulder.

"Right!" she told him, her voice too loud in the silence of the barn. "I'll get it."

The mix felt sticky between her fingers, its fragrant aroma curling up to greet her nostrils as she plunged her hand into the yellow bucket beside the feed bins. Sunny banged on his door, thump… thump… thump inside her head as her hand went around and around, mixing, mixing. Jumbled thoughts raced around her head, vying for her attention, Bess, nut brown and smiling, the sad, burned out cottage. There had to be a link…

"This horse of yours will knock the door down if you don't hurry up – and it's almost dark. Don't you think it's time you went home?"

Bob Atkins' voice brought her sharply back to the present. She grabbed the bucket and swung it around, glancing up at him apologetically while moving quickly across to where he was already opening Sunny's door.

"Sorry, I was miles away. What time is it?"

"Almost seven o' clock. Your mother will be frantic. We all thought you went home when Dillon came in an hour ago."

She shook her head, remembering the note on the kitchen table.

"No… I mean, I told him I was going but I just kind of got carried away brushing Sunny."

Bob crossed his arms over his chest, gazing appreciatively at the dun gelding's gleaming golden coat.

"Well you've certainly done a good job there, but honestly, don't you think that your mother will be worried?"

Sunny plunged his head into the yellow bucket, tossing it over in his eagerness to gobble the feed while the two cows observed, interested and patient. Tilly slid his stall door bolt home and stood up tall.

"She has a late meeting tonight. She won't be home until at least nine…"

She moved across toward the open doorway, staring out into the blackness of the night with a jolt of apprehension. Suddenly the idea of biking home all alone in the dark was less than appealing.

"Anyway…" She forced a smile onto her face. "It is a bit later than I thought. I'll see you tomorrow."

"Not so fast, young lady."

Bob Atkins ran his fingers down his chin, gripping the end of it between thumb and forefinger, his blue eyes narrowed.

"I can't have you biking home alone in the dead of night. What if something happened to you? Vee would never forgive me. No… Why don't you come inside for something to eat? Come on, throw your bike in the back of the pickup and I'll run you home when you've eaten."

Relief washed over Tilly in a wave that made her stomach churn… or was that just hunger? Her expression said it all.

"Thank you! I'll work extra hard tomorrow."

"Don't worry," responded Bob. "I'll make sure you do."

It was warm in the large farmhouse kitchen, warm and cozy and just so homely that Tilly felt a rush of emotion. Vague memories flooded over her, memories from before… She shook her head, dispersing them, and went across to where Dillon was already concentrating on the jigsaw.

"You haven't wasted much time," she remarked.

He replied without looking up.

"This jigsaw has waited long enough… just look for straight edges or corners. You have to get the outside done first, you see."

"I didn't realize you were such an expert," she laughed, pushing the pieces around the box. "Oh, here's one."

She passed him a corner piece and he pounced on it, placing it carefully into position. She glanced at the picture that was already taking place and a shiver ran down her spine. It was

99

all just too much to take in. How could he be sitting here, calmly making Elizabeth's jigsaw?"

"Come on," urged Vee Atkins, pushing a plate in front of her. "You haven't eaten since lunch."

Tilly looked around sharply to meet warm understanding in her soft brown eyes. She smiled impulsively and Vee smiled back.

"Tell me about it when you've eaten," she suggested, placing a comforting hand on Tilly's shoulder. "Everything looks better with a full stomach."

The sandwich was really more of a meal between two huge chunks of homemade bread, beef, thick and delicious, lettuce, tomato and a slathering of mayonnaise. Tilly munched happily, her spirits rising with every mouthful.

"You see," smiled Vee handing her a glass of milk. "I told you you'd feel better when you'd eaten."

"Thanks." Tilly wiped her mouth with the back of her hand. "It was all a bit traumatic... you know… this afternoon."

"Dillon did tell me something about it. It must have been sad to see the place where Elizabeth died."

"Do you think that there can be a link?"

There, she had said it; she had voiced the thought that had been with her all day, the idea that the two girls had something in common.

Vee raised her eyebrows and then lowered them again, before drawing them together into a concentrated frown.

"What… you mean a link between Elizabeth and Bess, the girl who helped you… how can there be? Elizabeth has been dead for twenty years at least."

Tilly lifted her head defiantly, unwilling to let her conviction slip away.

"They could be related," she suggested hopefully. "Elizabeth could be Bess's aunt or something."

Vee shrugged. "Who knows, but I doubt it. After his daughter

100

died Elizabeth's father disappeared. They say that he couldn't face the guilt, you know, about not being there when she died. No one ever saw him again. I don't remember there being any other relatives."

"But there might have been?"

Tilly stood up, waiting eagerly for Vee's response. To her disappointment she saw only shadows in Vee's eyes.

"Who knows?" she remarked briskly. "Now come on, time to stop brooding on the past. Bob will drive you home."

Dillon raised his head briefly as she called goodbye, flashing her an infectious grin.

"Don't forget, you promised me another lesson tomorrow," he reminded her, his eyes already wandering back toward the jigsaw.

"That's if you can drag yourself away," smiled Tilly.

He slipped another piece neatly into place.

"Oh it'll easily be finished by then."

"That," remarked his mother. "Remains to be seen. Didn't you say that you had some schoolwork to finish?"

As Bob's elderly pickup bounced uncomfortably along the lane Tilly stared out at the night sky. It seemed totally black, with not even one star to break its intensity, and yet the hedges on either side of the lane loomed blacker still. She clung to the sides of her seat, glad to be seeing the road from behind two powerful headlights – the beam from the light on her bike would have been no more than a pinprick in the gloom. Her thoughts kept trying to wander back to Crickle Wood and Elizabeth's cottage, but she forced the memories out, wanting to think of anything other than the day behind her. In doing so she sat in silence, unaware of Bob's concerned glance.

"You OK? He asked gruffly.

She smiled through the darkness, looking across to where the angular planes of his face were silhouetted against the glow of the headlights.

"Yes… And thanks for the lift. I didn't feel much like biking, to be honest."

"I should think not. You must try to get off a bit sooner now that the days are shorter."

They fell then into a companionable silence, until the pickup rattled to a halt.

"Here we are!" announced Bob, pulling on the handbrake. The engine settled into a steady rumble, breaking the silence of the night, and Tilly felt suddenly reluctant to step out into the shadows.

Tilly's house stood alone on the side of the narrow country road, a dark square shape against the night sky. She placed her fingers tentatively onto the door handle, looking uneasily across to where the windows glared out at her, black and lifeless.

"We should leave a light on," she remarked, clearing her throat.

"Don't worry…"

Detecting the tremble in her voice, Bob gave her arm a quick squeeze.

"Don't worry," he repeated. "I'll wait right here until you've switched *all* the lights on."

"Thanks…"

She pulled on the handle, the pickup door opened with a creak, and she turned back to smile in his general direction.

"It is a bit scary going into a dark house by yourself."

He leaned forward impulsively.

"Do you want me to come in with you, you know, just to make sure everything's alright?"

"No… thanks."

From having spent the last few hours desperately trying to force the events of the afternoon out of her mind, suddenly

Tilly realized that she wanted to embrace them. She needed to be alone for a while, to get things straight inside her head. Her hand pushed determinedly against the door and a rush of cold night air took her breath away.

"I'll be fine now... and thanks again for the ride. "

She clambered clumsily out of the vehicle, raising her hand in farewell as she turned toward the cottage. True to his word Bob waited with the engine running until she had unlocked the front door and illuminated the whole place with light. It wasn't until he revved the pickup engine and disappeared with a farewell honk of the horn that she remembered her bike. It seemed that she would have to set off for Cricklewood Farm especially early tomorrow.

The kitchen was warm with the heat of the wood stove, warm and homey and very safe. Tilly felt as if she could really concentrate on the traumas of the afternoon now. Her mother had left supper on a plate in the fridge, but she couldn't even think about food. She put milk in a saucepan to heat for cocoa, sank down onto the chair nearest to the stove and allowed her mind to drift. Bess in the woods that day, brave and strong, like a woodland creature herself. Elizabeth must have been like that, brave and strong. She died fighting for her horse's life after all, how noble was that? She imagined herself in the same situation. Sunny screaming out his fear as the flames licked against his stable door. Oh why hadn't Elizabeth just opened the door and chased him out? Did anyone ever really find out the truth about that night? Would anyone ever really know exactly how she died? A thought suddenly occurred to her, a scary and exciting thought. She would go and look at the paper for the day after Elizabeth died. Surely the Cricklewood Gazette must have run quite a story. Did they keep papers for twenty years?

Her mind raced around in circles as she sipped her cocoa. She would go to the Gazette office tomorrow, she decided, and just ask if she could look at their back copies of the newspaper – but would they let her?

A sound broke the silence, the clink of a key in the front door lock. She jumped up, disorientated, glancing at the wall clock. Nine thirty. Where had the evening gone?

"Tilda!"

Her mother's voice floated through from the hallway and relief rushed in. Mom would understand, she would know what to do.

"You wouldn't believe the day I've had…!"

Fenna burst through the kitchen door, her usually pale face bright with color and her arms bulging with an assortment of books. She released them onto the pine table with a flourish.

"Enter the new me!" she exclaimed, throwing her arms up in the air.

Tilly frowned.

"What happened to the old you? I kind of liked her."

"Matilda, my dear, it's time to move on. I've spent long enough brooding over what might have been, and now I'm going to shape my own destiny… Look!"

She lifted up a book, and pointed at the title.

"You see, English Literature. That's what I'm going to be studying. Well, I mean, one of the things I'll be studying."

Tilly stood quite still, her jaw slowly dropping.

"Studying!"

"Yes, studying," declared Fenna. "Your father's living abroad and you're always busy doing your own thing on the farm. I need a complete change, some time for me."

A knot twisted in Tilly's stomach.

"Do you think he'll ever come back?"

Fenna's gray eyes softened.

"I'm sorry, honey. I know he loves you, it's just…"

Tilly wrapped her arms around herself as anger flooded in.

104

"That's why you're being like this, isn't it?"

The color drained from her mother's face and she placed the book gently back down onto the table.

"Like what?"

"All strong and independent. It's not really you, Mom."

"No? Well, we'll see about that. I'll show him. I've enrolled in a college course and I'm going to study to be a teacher."

"See," remarked Tilly sadly. "I said it was all about him."

Fenna placed a hand on her daughter's shoulder.

"Oh, come on, hon," she pleaded. "Don't be like that. Be happy for me. It's what I want."

For a moment there was silence in the room, broken only by the loud, rhythmic ticking of the wall clock, and then suddenly Tilly smiled.

"My Mom… a teacher," she announced.

"That's me," giggled Fenna, twirling around in a circle, excitement coloring her face as she looked cautiously at her daughter.

Despite herself, Tilly felt laughter gurgling up inside. "Sometimes I feel as if you're the daughter and I'm the Mom," she grumbled.

"And you're not too upset about your dad…?"

"I suppose he'll be back when he's ready," she sighed. Suddenly Crickle Wood and its long ago tragedy seemed less important than it had an hour ago. She decided she would find a better moment to talk to her mother about it.

Fenna bustled about the kitchen, talking constantly about her plans and Tilly was so pleased to see her in such good spirits again that somehow the "moment" never came. As she undressed and slipped beneath the soft coolness of her covers she realized that it was too late now to ask for her mother's advice. Fenna would still be asleep when she left in the morning, and long gone before she came home for breakfast.

No, this was something she would just have to do alone. At least there was no school tomorrow.

She snuggled down in the darkness, waiting for sleep to drift her off into oblivion. Memories raced around and around inside her head of the poor sad cottage completely taken over by nature, and the stable, oh the stable. Shuddering, she pulled the covers tightly around her, not wanting to think of the awful fate of the poor, defenseless horse and his brave, heroic mistress.

Had Elizabeth's father ever set foot in the cottage again? She wondered. The furniture had just been left to rot, and the jigsaw… oh, how she wished that Dillon had left it where it was, deep in the cupboard. It was unnerving to see just how much the picture on the box had looked like her and Sunny. What if… She shook her head to try to remove the crazy thought that had just slipped into her mind, a thought that made her shiver despite the warm comfort of her bed. It was almost twenty years since Elizabeth's death, her anniversary, and the jigsaw had lain untouched for all that time. What if something weird happened when Dillon finally completed it?

Leaping out of bed with her heart thumping she rushed to switch on the light, absorbing the familiar sight of her room.

"You are crazy, Matilda McCloud," she announced out loud to the mirror. Her face stared back at her, white and colorless, gray eyes wide as if with shock.

"And you don't look anything like the girl in the stupid jigsaw," she added. Suddenly everything clicked back into place. She had been overly imaginative as usual, that's all, and gotten everything completely out of perspective. But she *would* go to the Gazette office tomorrow anyway, she decided, just to find out the truth about Elizabeth. Somehow she felt that she owed her that.

Tilly's new calm perspective on things lasted until she reached Cricklewood Farm the next morning.

"Morning," called Bob as she walked through the gate.

"Morning," she responded with a grin.

Hearing her voice from his stable inside the barn, Sunny whinnied, a loud ringing neigh that echoed through the crisp autumn air. Bob stopped and looked across at her, hammer in one hand and saw in the other.

"He's been making a fuss since early on," he told her. "I went to check on him half an hour ago but he was fine. Just missing you, I guess."

At that moment Dillon's tall, lanky figure appeared through the orchard gate. He held out his boot, staring at it ruefully.

"That darned Roger may not have any spurs left, but he's still just as determined to get me," he groaned.

"You should try being nice to him," suggested Tilly. "You know, always have a tidbit in your pocket, and make a fuss over him instead of chasing him off."

"Wring his neck is more like it," grumbled Dillon. Sunny's loud neigh rang out from the barn again, cutting off their conversation and he raised his hands skyward. "Wring his neck too, if he doesn't shut up. He's been doing that all morning. In fact…" his face lit up with mischievous grin. "It was kind of weird…"

Tilly's mouth went dry.

"What was weird?"

"Well… I spent all yesterday evening doing that stupid jigsaw puzzle, but I couldn't seem to make the last few pieces fit. Anyway, when I was having breakfast first thing this morning I looked at it again, and it all just seemed to click."

"Typical," groaned Bob, walking off across the yard, hammer and saw held aloft. "I'm already out working and you're doing a jigsaw puzzle."

Dillon ignored him.

"I just picked up the pieces of Sunny's head," he went on, "and they kind of fell into place. In fact, it was as he looked out at me from the picture that I first heard him neigh, and he's been doing it ever since…"

He looked at Tilly with a self-satisfied expression on his face and she stepped determinedly forward, trying to ignore the fluttering feeling that made her stomach churn.

"What a load of trash you talk, Dillon Atkins," she exclaimed. "What are you trying to tell me… that there's some kind of strange link between Sunny and Elizabeth's jigsaw? And I thought I was over-imaginative! Anyway, I don't remember feeling odd when you finished the bit that looks like me."

"Ah…" He raised his eyebrows and gave her a gentle push. "But you were probably asleep in your bed then. How do you feel now? Come on, think about it."

Tilly pushed him back hard and marched off across the yard as he struggled to find his balance.

"I feel that *you* are totally crazy," she told him. "And I am going to feed Sunny."

"Don't forget about my lesson," he called after her.

Sunny was staring toward the door with shining amber eyes. He nickered when he saw Tilly appear, stretching his neck over the wooden partition that made up one side of his stable, and twisting his head to one side.

"So you think you look appealing, do you?" she laughed. He tossed his head and she ran her hand down his face, pressing her lips against his velvety nose.

"Now, what is it that's bugging you, boy?" she asked. In response he whinnied again, a loud ringing cry that made her put her hands over her ears.

"Hey… hey… hey…! Do you know something I don't? Come on," she grabbed a yellow bucket and made for the feed bin. "I know what you want."

Five minutes later he was munching ecstatically on his feed while Tilly deftly threw back his straw bed, separating the soiled parts and piling the clean straw against the wall. As he finished his last mouthful and looked up for more she stood back to gaze at her handiwork with satisfaction. Gleaming golden straw, perfectly rolled banks.

"Well I have to admit it's not a *bad* job," remarked Dillon from behind her.

"Better than you could do," she laughed.

"Well that is something we will never know because I certainly don't ever intend to try," he retorted. "Now, about my riding lesson…"

"And you think you deserve one after trying to frighten me this morning?"

"Ah…" He stood back, nodding his head. "So you do think that there's something strange about the jigsaw."

She closed the stable door, placed her fork carefully against the wall and took the head collar from its peg on the wall.

"I am not even going to answer that ridiculous question," she replied, slipping it over Sunny's head. "Anyway, it depends what your father has planned for us today, because I have to go into Cricklewood this afternoon."

Dillon fell in beside her as she led the big dun gelding out of his box and across the yard toward the meadow beside the lane… the meadow where Bess told her that the Atkinses turned out their horses.

"Do you remember the horses your mother use to have?" she asked suddenly.

"Give me a break," cried Dillon. "I know I'm pretty amazing, but even I can't remember things from before I was born."

Tilly led Sunny through the gate, turned him toward it and slipped the head collar over his ears.

"Well…"

She stood still for a moment, watching proudly as he galloped off across the spongy turf, bucking and leaping. "I don't know who told you that you were amazing, but I think you should let them know that they couldn't have been more wrong."

She walked back out into the lane and as Dillon closed the gate carefully behind her his whole face puckered into a comical expression of disbelief.

"What… you don't think I'm amazing?"

"Definitely not," she giggled, breaking into a run. "And I bet I'll be first back into the yard."

They sprinted around the corner of the barn, neck and neck, shrieking with laughter as they vied for first place. The sight of Bob Atkins standing beside the pickup truck with a stern expression on his face pulled them up instantly.

"I've been looking for you two," he grumbled. "I have an appointment in town in twenty minutes, and I want to tell you what to get on with this morning."

"Go on, then," said Dillon. "Tell us what delights we have in store today."

Tilly stood watching as Bob gave his son a list of orders, but her thoughts were far away from chickens and Cricklewood Farm. Apprehension made her nerve ends tingle as she remembered her plan to visit the Gazette office this afternoon. Should she go through with it? A vision of the burned out stable in the wood filled her mind again, and the sad, neglected cottage, where poor Elizabeth had once lived. Was it really her jigsaw Dillon had found? It must have been. She had probably placed it in that cupboard, intending to make it one day, not knowing that tragedy would prevent her from ever even starting it. A lump formed in her throat and she blinked hard. Yes, she decided, she would go to try to find out more. Whether or not she was related to *her* Bess, Elizabeth at least deserved that.

"Come on then, dreamer," urged Dillon, nudging her in the ribs. "We'll be at this all day if we don't shape up, and you have to give me another riding lesson, remember."

"I told you," Tilly's voice was sharper than she intended. "I have to go at lunch time."

"Sorry for breathing," retorted Dillon.

"Oh, don't worry," she laughed apologetically. "I'll give you a lesson before I leave. If we have time, that is."

"I haven't told you what my dad wants us to do yet," he replied sheepishly.

"Well…" She looked up at him with a puzzled frown. "It can't be all that bad, surely."

He hesitated for a moment, an impish grin lighting up his larger than life features.

"It depends on how you look at, it I suppose."

"Go on," she groaned.

"We only have to clean out *Roger's* chicken coop," he exclaimed, raising his hands skywards.

"That's OK," giggled Tilly. "It's you he doesn't like… especially since you cut off his spurs."

Half an hour later Dillon heaved the last shovelful into the wheelbarrow and stood up, his hand resting on the small of his back.

"I don't want to have to do that again for a while," he exclaimed.

"Oh, I don't know," retorted Tilly with a smile. "I didn't think it was too bad."

"Maybe that's because you didn't actually do anything."

She picked up the shovel and brush, heaving them across her shoulder.

"Well it's only a small pen, so we could hardly both get inside. And I did keep Roger away from you, remember."

"And I suppose I'm the one who's going to have to push this

up the hill," grumbled Dillon, picking up the handles of the laden wheelbarrow.

"OK, point taken."

Tilly patted him sympathetically on the shoulder and set off across the orchard.

"I'll go and bring Sunny in; you can have that lesson as a reward for your hard work… but watch out!"

Following her gaze he looked around to see Roger racing toward him, wings outstretched and beady eyes glaring.

The sight of him, pushing the heavy wheelbarrow over the rough grass with the mottled gray rooster on his heels brought tears of laughter to Tilly's eyes. She was still laughing as she walked across the meadow to catch Sunny, and she giggled all through the arduous task of brushing the sticky mud from his golden coat.

She breathed in his warm, horsy aroma, reveling in the sight of the glorious shine that her efforts were gradually revealing. Elizabeth and Bess and the burned out stable in the center of the wood seemed a lifetime away.

"Do you think I'm just being crazy, boy?" she murmured, pressing her cheek against his silken neck. He turned to push her gently with his nose and she let out a deep sigh.

Twenty minutes later Dillon eased back on the reins and looked across at Tilly, an ecstatic smile lighting up what she secretly thought of as his puppy dog features.

"How am I doing?" he called.

"Well…."

She frowned, rubbing her chin.

"You need to sit up a bit straighter, and your heels keep creeping up, but, unbelievably, you are doing pretty well."

"Honestly…?

His face glowed with pride.

"Do you really think so?"

Tilting her head to one side, Tilly pursed her lips thoughtfully, and then grinned.

"Well… at least… considering that it is only your second lesson."

"So do you think I'm ready to try a canter?"

His expression was so appealing that she didn't have the heart to refuse him.

"Not really, but if you feel confident enough then I suppose you could try. Just remember to let your hips swing with Sunny's back, a bit like when he walks, but much, much more."

Dillon gently nudged the dun gelding's sides and he moved eagerly forward.

"That's it," called Tilly. "Go with him, get your rising trot right and wait for the corner."

Sensing his rider's lack of balance Sunny steadied obligingly.

"Now in the next corner just sit down and give him a squeeze."

A lump formed in her throat as she watched them bound into canter. Sunny's ears pricked sharply forward, his mane rising and falling on his neck in the sunshine, and Dillon sat so tall and proud.

"You're a natural," she told him when he reined in beside her. His face beamed with pleasure and she laughed.

"Now come on. I have to go, remember."

"Not before you've looked at the jigsaw," insisted Dillon as he slipped to the ground.

"Oh, yes…" murmured Tilly. "The jigsaw."

She placed the palm of her hand against her stomach as it churned uncomfortably, and another, an invisible hand, seemed to squeeze at her heart.

"Maybe I could see it tomorrow…"

"Now," insisted Dillon, grabbing hold of her arm. "It'll only take a minute."

The hand around her heart squeezed tighter when Tilly's eyes settled on the table beside the window. For the girl who looked out at her – despite the intricate patterns made by the pieces of the jigsaw – had an uncomfortable familiarity with the face that stared at her in the mirror each morning.

"See," announced Dillon, folding his arms across his chest. "I told you."

"OK… so she looks a bit like me… But the horse is nothing like Sunny."

He frowned crossly. Sure enough the horse that stood beside the girl in the picture was a kind of golden brown, but it was smaller that Sunny, more of a pony.

"But don't you think it's weird that we just happen to have found a jigsaw of someone who looks like you?" he asked.

"I think it's kind of weird that we found it at all," murmured Tilly uncomfortably. "Elizabeth must have intended to make it herself… and then she was killed, and twenty years later it's you who has made it."

"Well, I think it's nice that someone actually finished it for her," insisted Dillon. "I just find it a bit of a strange coincidence that she picked a picture that looks just like you in the first place."

A shiver rippled down Tilly's spine. Suddenly she wanted to be anywhere but here.

"Well, I'm off," she announced, heading for the door. "I'll see you later on."

"See you," echoed Dillon, his eyes still firmly fixed on the jigsaw.

chapter nine

Tilly walked through the gate to Millside cottage and into the lane, desperately trying to hang on to the determination she had managed to muster as she pedaled home at lunchtime. Over to her left Burnbrook village nestled beneath the hills, and to her right Crickle Wood stretched along beside the river almost to the edges of Cricklewood town. The farm was in the other direction, a mile or so to the east. She hesitated in the edge of the narrow, overgrown lane, looking longingly toward it. Sunny would be standing in his stable now, picking at his hay net, bored and restless. Oh, how she longed to go and take him out for a ride. Perhaps she should just forget about her stupid quest.

Above her head, high up in the branches of an old oak tree, a bird burst into song, loud and clear in the cool crisp air. She followed its path as it flew away, over the treetops that were slowly turning to flame. From green to red and glorious gold the whole of Crickle Wood was basking in autumn glory… an autumn glory that poor Elizabeth would never see. Suddenly her quest seemed important again. She lifted her chin and headed toward the bus stop at the end of the lane… but what if they wouldn't let her look at the old newspapers?

"What if… what if… what if…." she murmured to herself as she saw the cumbersome red bus approach.

Minutes later she was on her way, swaying and bouncing along the road. Was she wasting her time, she wondered? After all, even if she did get to read the newspaper story about the fire in the wood, how could it tell her whether or not Elizabeth and Bess were related? She didn't even know Bess's last name.

The Gazette office nestled on the very edge of the main street of the market town, between a butcher shop and a jeweler. Unaltered for a hundred years or more, it seemed a quaint, old-fashioned place, and Tilly's confidence grew as she marched down its long narrow interior toward the counter at the very far end.

"Yes?"

A tall thin woman peered down her nose through half moon spectacles, her pen poised in her hand.

Tilly cleared her throat.

"I wondered if I could look at some of your back copies, please."

The woman put down her pen and frowned.

"You'll have to bring an adult with you, I'm afraid. Get one of your parents to call and arrange it for you… Sorry."

She turned her attention back to the form she was filling out and Tilly looked at the ground feeling totally despondent. What a waste of an afternoon. She couldn't just give up so easily.

"Please…" she begged. "Couldn't you make an exception just this once? It is for a school project… a very important school project."

The woman looked up, her forehead puckered into an irritated frown.

"No," she barked. "I can't allow…"

"Hey… hey… hey. What have we here?" interrupted another voice. Tilly looked around to see an elderly gentleman standing beside her. His lined face was creased into a smile, and beneath a mop of snow-white hair his blue eyes peered at her in a friendly fashion. Hope soared and she seized her chance.

116

"I have a school project about events from twenty years ago, and I want to look at the papers from then," she pleaded. "It's really important and I have to finish it today."

"Well, young lady, it seems that you are in luck," he announced. "I happen to be writing a book about past events in Cricklewood, based on the stories told in the Gazette."

He paused and looked sternly at the pinched face of the woman on the other side of the counter.

"I'm sure that Miss Thomas wouldn't object if I accompany you."

She squirmed and looked away.

"Well, you will have to take full responsibility for her..."

"I'm sure I can take that risk," he smiled, urging Tilly forward. "Come along my dear... My name is Peter Rawcliffe, by the way."

"Thank you," she responded with a smile. "And I'm Matilda. Matilda McCloud, but everyone calls me Tilly."

She followed him down a narrow staircase and into a long storeroom, where he was obviously well at home.

"Now," he urged. "What exactly are we looking for?"

She had only to mention the fire in Crickle Wood and he knew exactly what date it happened.

"The twenty first of October," he exclaimed. "Almost twenty-one years ago to the day. In fact tomorrow night will be the twenty first anniversary of the whole sorry business."

"Do you remember it?" cried Tilly, but he shook his head.

"No, it happened just before I moved here. I came as a teacher, to Cricklewood High. Long retired now, of course. I have read about it, though... terrible tragedy. Such a waste."

He rifled methodically through the newspapers until he found the one he wanted, spreading it out carefully onto the table. Tilly felt suddenly hot and cold. Breathlessly she looked at the front page.

The figure in the photograph jumped out at her; remarkably clear, considering its age… a figure that could have been Bess herself. She was smiling, her arm draped across the neck of a sturdy colored cob. Domino? Was it Domino? *No… no… don't be ridiculous*, she told herself. Her heart filled her ears, suffocating her senses as she fought for composure.

"There she is," remarked Peter Rawcliffe sadly. "Elizabeth Malone. What a waste of a young life… and the poor horse."

Malone… Malone… Malone… The words circled around and around in Tilly's head. Where had she heard that name before?

Her eyes devoured the writing on the page, taking in every detail of the tragic story…

When a fire raged in a stable deep in the center of Crickle Wood last night, a young girl lost her life trying to save her beloved horse. The cause of the fire is yet unknown, but by the time the alarm was raised it was already too late for fifteen-year-old Elizabeth Malone and the horse she gave her life for. It is believed that the fire started in a small hay store attached to the stable. Elizabeth Malone and her horse both died when the roof of the stable collapsed while she was trying to save the four-year-old gelding that she had owned since he was just six months old. Mr. Malone, Elizabeth's father, was not available for comment this morning…

The words began to swim before Tilly's eyes. A roaring sound filled her head, and for a moment she held onto the edge of the table, breathing deeply. When she eventually looked up Peter Rawcliffe's blue eyes were narrowed with concern.

"Are you all right?" he asked urgently.

She smiled vaguely, nodding her head like a puppet.

"Yes… yes… it's just. I think I know one of Elizabeth's relatives, and they look so alike..."

He frowned, shaking his head slowly.

"Well, I know that her father moved away after the tragedy, but I haven't heard of any other relatives. You'll have to introduce me."

Suddenly Tilly needed to get as far away as possible from the face that stared out at her, for an idea that was dawning in her mind was just too much to take in. What if Bess, the friend she so much wanted to meet again, was the ghost of long dead Elizabeth… and Domino? No, it couldn't be. She stood up, scraping back her chair.

"Thank you… Thank you for helping me…"

"Well, if there's anything else you need to research?"

"Research...?"

She stared at him vacantly.

"For your project…" he prompted.

"Oh… oh, yes. I'll let you know."

As Tilly ran off up the stairs to the main office again, the tall white haired man watched her rapid retreat with a puzzled expression in his blue eyes, before going back to read the story that had caused her so much consternation. As far as he was aware Elizabeth had been an only child who lived alone with her father. He would do a little research himself, he decided, just to see if she did have any other relatives. It had seemed so important to the girl to find out. And if anything came to light he would let her know.

The late afternoon sun hung over the top of the hill that loomed beyond Crickle Wood, a golden, glowing orb of light.

119

Tilly stood quite still in the lengthening shadows. Her mind was a mile away from Cricklewood Farm or Dillon, or even Sunny. All she could think of was the face that stared out at her from the paper, Bess's face. She couldn't seem to get past the vision of the girl who looked so like her friend, the friend who had stepped forward that day and saved them from galloping straight onto the main road. Why had no one been there to help Elizabeth? It seemed so wrong. And Domino, dear, sweet, gentle Domino. To have perished in the flames like that... But it wasn't Domino, was it? She stifled a sob, pushing her fist hard against her mouth.

"Hey hey hey..."

Dillon materialized beside her, his usually pleasant features showing deep concern.

"What's wrong...?"

She looked up to meet his blue eyes through a blur of tears.

"I went to the Gazette office today," she mumbled.

He frowned, shaking his head.

"To read about the tragedy in the wood," she explained.

Clarity dawned and he nodded, placing an arm around her shoulders to give her an awkward hug.

"It was twenty years ago," he reminded her. "And you have to get this stupid idea out of your head that Elizabeth was somehow related to your Bess."

"But what if...?" Tilly hardly dared to voice the crazy notion that kept coming back into her mind.

"What if what?"

"What if Bess and Domino were ghosts..." There, she had said it.

Dillon's response was unexpected. He burst into hoots of laughter and pulled her around to face him.

"Now I know that you really have lost it, Matilda call me Tilly McCloud," he grinned. "Come on, get a grip. You'll

120

find her soon, you'll see, and then you'll laugh at your crazy imagination. Bess and her horse will definitely come back to Crickle Wood eventually, believe me. Anyway…"

He took her by both shoulders and stared straight into her face.

"Forget about something that happened twenty years ago. I have something much more important to tell you."

She blinked away her tears, feeling suddenly selfish and more than a bit stupid.

"Sorry… it's just my stupid imagination working overtime again. Go on…"

His eyes were alight with excitement, and a broad grin spread slowly across his face.

"My dad has found me a horse."

"A horse… your own horse? What, just like that?"

"That's my dad for you," he laughed. "He doesn't mess around."

"But when, and how…?"

Confusion rushed in as Tilly tried to get her head back into now. Dillon was to have his own horse… a companion for Sunny…. someone to ride with. Excitement bubbled, chasing away her fears.

"He's a black and white four-year-old gelding, about sixteen hands high, and he's being delivered tomorrow."

"And you haven't even seen him?"

Dillon shook his head.

"It was all just a bit of a coincidence. My dad was at a farm sale today and he saw the horse in a field. Bill Jackson, the farmer who was retiring, said that he didn't want to put it through the sale as he had bred it himself and he didn't want it going just anywhere. Anyway, Dad persuaded him to let us take it on trial, and if it works out we can talk about buying it."

"Wow!" cried Tilly.

"And so you'll help me with him…?"

She looked up at him, all trace of tears completely gone. "Just try stopping me," she laughed.

Sunny stood with eyes half closed, enjoying the feel of the body brush sweeping across his coat and totally unaware of the emotions racing through his mistress's mind. Tomorrow night was the anniversary of the tragedy in the wood. It preyed on her mind, always there, even though she kept on reminding herself of Dillon's advice. Something that happened years ago, before she was even born, really had nothing to do with her, and she didn't honestly believe that Bess was a ghost… did she? So why did it feel so important, as if it had affected her personally?

She eased her arm around the inside of Sunny's hind leg, cupping the hoof, ready with the hoof pick. As usual he slammed his foot down before she was finished and she let out an exasperated cry.

"You'll have to do better than that when my four-year-old comes," remarked Dillon. "Here, let me try."

"It's the one thing he does that really annoys me," she exclaimed, handing him the hoof pick.

"That and putting your life in danger by bolting toward main roads."

"Oh yes, there is that as well," she smiled as he neatly picked out Sunny's foot and placed it back down into the straw. "…Now how did you do that? I'm supposed to be the experienced one."

Handing her the hoof pick, he shrugged.

"Animals are all the same, I guess. You just have to be firm and let them know who's in charge. Sunny knows he can snatch his foot away from you so he does it. If you hang on a bit harder and show him that he can't, he'll give in…"

"A bit like you with Roger, I suppose."

"Yeah," he responded. "A bit like that… As I said, you just have to show them who's boss. It has to do with the pecking order…"

"And you are… where… on *Roger's* pecking order?" she giggled.

Suddenly they were both laughing out loud and all her worries magically faded. The tragedy in the wood seemed a lifetime ago… *was* a lifetime ago.

"So where are you going to stable him?" she asked eagerly, her mind full of Dillon's new horse.

"Well, we thought…" he began, as she closed the door of the barn.

"Come and get a slice of the cake I just baked before you set off for home," called Vee from the back porch, and side-by-side Tilly and Dillon tramped across the yard, deep in excited conversation about their plans for both the new horse and Sunny.

"I'd like to show jump him," remarked Dillon as they walked into the comfortable warmth of the kitchen.

Tilly wrinkled her nose at the enticing aroma of cake, fresh from the oven.

"You'd better learn to walk before you can run," she advised.

"Don't you mean canter before you can jump?" he laughed.

"Something like that."

"It might be a good idea if you learn to ride properly before you start making such ambitious plans," suggested his mother. "Now sit yourselves down and I'll get you both a hot chocolate."

Tilly slept deeply and easily that night, determined as she was to think ahead instead of back into the distant past. Her thoughts were full of horses, living horses, Sunny and the new black and white four-year-old. It was only as her eyelids drooped that she allowed her mind to turn toward Bess and Domino. She longed to tell her elusive friend all about Cricklewood Farm and Dillon and his new horse. After all, if it hadn't been for Bess she would have never even gone there in the first place. And did she really believe that she and Domino could be ghosts? A picture of Bess flashed into her mind, strong and stalwart, standing in the center of the pathway as Sunny galloped toward her. No… Dillon was right; the idea was ridiculous. "One day I'll find you," she murmured as sleep overtook her.

She woke only once. As the moon filtered in through her window, long before dawn peered over the horizon, she half opened her eyes, ears tuned to a distant cry. Her mind fought to take in the echoing call, but slumber closed around her again, drawing her back under its comforting blanket. There was just one more moment, between sleeping and waking, when she remembered the call with an ache of regret, and then her mother's voice was floating up the stairs and panic closed in. She was late.

"Matilda! Come on! It's a good thing there's no school today."

She leaped out of bed and ran into the bathroom, scrubbing her teeth with one hand while dragging on her jodhpurs with the other. When she raced down the stairs two at a time Fenna already had her breakfast ready.

"I can't believe that you slept later than I," she cried as her daughter burst into the kitchen.

"Well, you do get up sooner than you used to," Tilly reminded her. "Now that you have a new focus in your life."

Fenna smiled. "Yes I suppose I have, haven't I?"

"You will save a bit of time for me though, won't you?"

Her mother's eyebrows rose indignantly.

"Matilda McCloud, I will always find time for you… if I can find you in the first place, of course."

Tilly took a spoonful of cereal. "Well I suppose you have made my breakfast," she grinned, munching happily. "But you weren't here last night when I wanted to tell you about yesterday."

"I was at my evening class, you know I was. Anyway, what about yesterday? Tell me now."

Tilly hesitated, thinking about her trip to the Gazette office and Dillon's new horse.

"I'll tell you tonight," she promised, slipping on her jacket. "They'll wonder where I've gone."

Dillon and Tilly raced around all morning, trying to get all their chores done before the new horse came at lunchtime. Bluebell and Daffodil had been relegated to a pen at the other end of the barn so that he could be stabled next to Sunny, but it took ten barrow loads to clear out the old bed of straw. Tilly held her aching back as she split a bale of shavings and spread them around, banking them up against the walls. When the bed was smoothed out to her satisfaction she stood back with a critical eye.

"You'll have to put Sunny on shavings instead of straw," suggested Dillon. "I know that straw looks nice but he eats far too much of it, and as Dad has managed to get hold of these cheap shavings..."

"I'll do it tomorrow," she said absentmindedly. I suppose he is getting a bit fat."

"A bit!" shrieked Dillon.

She reached across to hit him but he jumped out of her reach.

"Don't take any notice of him," she advised Sunny as he stretched his neck over the door, intrigued by their antics.

"The truck is here," called Bob Atkins from outside in the yard, and together they hurried out into the autumn sunshine.

The horse was bigger built that Tilly had expected. He looked more than sixteen hands and he had silky feather on his heels and a huge crest. He looked straight at them as he marched confidently down the ramp, big, honest eyes shining with anticipation.

"Domino!" she cried. "He looks like a bigger version of Domino…"

The elderly man who proudly held the lead-rope with gnarled, arthritic fingers, smiled across at her, his pale eyes surprisingly bright against the wrinkled parchment of his skin.

"Domino! Which Domino?"

It was Dillon who replied.

"Don't take any notice," he laughed, stepping forward. "Tilly has been trying to find a girl that she met in the woods a few weeks ago. She had a black and white cob called Domino and seemingly this fellow looks just like him."

"But bigger," interrupted Tilly. "He's bigger than Domino."

The old man held out his spare hand and took hold of Dillon's, pumping it up and down with a strength that belied his frail appearance.

"Bill Jackson," he announced. "And you must be Dillon…"

He turned then to smile at Tilly.

"Well, I'm afraid that I don't know the girl you're looking for," he told her. "This chap is related to a black and white cob called Domino, though, but that is no help to you either."

Tilly looked at him quizzically, heart racing.

He narrowed his eyes and sighed, thinking back.

"It was one I bred years ago; his sire will be this horse's grandsire. He's long gone though, I'm afraid. The poor thing died in a fire years ago."

Tilly felt her blood run cold.

"Twenty-one years ago to the day," she murmured.

"Must be at least that," remarked the old man. "Still, no point hanging on to the past."

Despite his excitement about his horse Dillon noticed the confusion on Tilly's face.

"Domino is a very common name for a black and white horse, you know," he reminded her. "So don't start up with any of your crazy ideas."

Tilly knew, in her heart of hearts she knew, that what the old man had said was the truth. This horse really was distantly related to the one that Elizabeth had died trying to save. Strangely, it made her feel better to think that his blood lived on, but it was just so uncannily weird that he had been called Domino too.

"It's OK," she said, smiling. "You're right, Domino is a common name for a black and white horse, and anyway, I like the idea that he kind of… you know… lives on."

"Well, thank heavens for that," hooted Dillon as he walked across to take the horse's lead rope. "You are seeing sense at last."

"Come on, Bill," suggested Bob Atkins. "The youngsters will see to the horse. Lets go and get a cup of tea and you can tell me how your farm sale went."

"But you haven't told us his name," called Tilly to their re-treating figures.

Bill Jackson looked back with a grin.

"Never got around to giving him a name," he said. "You'll have to think of one."

As Tilly and Dillon walked toward the barn with the big black and white gelding ambling happily along behind them, their minds were whirling.

"I've got it," exclaimed Dillon as Tilly opened the door. "And it's perfect."

"Go on, then," she smiled.

"I'm going to call him Jigsaw."

For a moment her heart fluttered.

"Jigsaw?" she echoed.

128

"Well, it fits, doesn't it? We found the jigsaw in the woods, there's a link between him and Elizabeth's Domino, and his patches look like the pieces of a jigsaw."

"I suppose so," agreed Tilly uneasily. "Isn't it weird, though, how things all seem to interlink. You know, Jigsaw's being related to Elizabeth's horse and finding out that he had the same name as Bess's Domino."

"You're not getting that ghost idea back into your head, are you?" he asked cautiously.

"No… no of course not. It's just that there are so many co-incidences."

"That, Matilda McCloud, is called life," offered Dillon gravely.

chapter ten

It had been a good day, reflected Tilly, as she adjusted Sunny's rug and checked his water bucket. He blew through his nostrils, a gentle, satisfying sound in the mellow silence of late afternoon. From the stable next door came an answering nicker, and when Jigsaw's large head appeared over the dividing wall she went across to rub his forehead.

"You are going to like your new home," she told him, breathing in his warm, horsy aroma. His coat felt rough beneath her fingers.

"And we'll soon have you looking just as glossy as Sunny," she promised.

They had tried the big black and white gelding that afternoon, just for fifteen minutes. Bill Jackson had advised them to leave him to settle in until the next day, but he seemed so relaxed in his new surroundings that they just couldn't resist tacking him up and riding him around the meadow.

Dillon had insisted that Tilly try him first.

"It's no good putting a novice like me on until we've seen what he's like," he said, and it did make sense. As she mounted up a shiver of excitement made her heart flutter. His fluffy ears flicked back once, and then he responded to her signals and ambled happily forward, broad and comfortable; very dependable, she decided.

"He feels great," she cried after her second circuit of the meadow. "Here…"

She slipped to the ground, patted his thick neck, and handed the reins to Dillon.

"He's your horse… you try him."

It made her heart ache to watch Dillon's expression. He looked so proud of himself.

"You're a natural," she called.

He flashed her a grin as he trotted by.

"I must have had a good teacher."

Smiling to herself at the memory she gave Sunny one last pat, called goodbye to Jigsaw and closed the barn door behind her, bolting it carefully before walking across to get her bicycle.

"See you tomorrow," called Dillon from the direction of the back door.

"See you," she responded with a wave, before setting off down the lane.

The autumn sunshine lent trees and hedges a crimson glow. Clear, crisp air filled her nostrils, and her legs ached comfortably as she pumped the pedals up and down. Funny how things seemed to work out, she thought. Finding the Atkinses, and Jigsaw being related to Elizabeth's Domino, as if everything kind of fit together. In fact, it seemed that life was like a jigsaw, everything fitting together. But what if a piece got lost?

Stupid idea, she told herself, quickening her pace. Suddenly the idea of home was very appealing, and she found herself hoping that her mother would be in tonight. It would be good to talk to her for once. Memories of the long chats she used to have with her father clouded her horizon and she increased her pace. Oh, why couldn't everything just have stayed as it was? Maybe things happened for a reason, though; if her father had been here she would have never gone to Cricklewood Farm in the first place. Yes, she decided, life *was* like a jigsaw, an intricate complicated jigsaw with every piece carefully slotting into place.

✧ ✧ ✧ ✧ ✧

Fenna McCloud hummed to herself as she ran a brush through her silky fair hair.

"I wish you weren't going out tonight," cried Tilly. She was perched on the side of her mother's bed, hands on her knees and eyebrows drawn into a disappointed frown.

Fenna turned her head to one side, viewing her profile.

"It's hardly out," she exclaimed. "More of an errand, really. I'll only be an hour or so… you can come with me if you like."

Tilly shook her head.

"It's OK…" she smiled. "I'm just being silly."

Silence fell between them then. Fenna carefully applied her makeup while Tilly's mind drifted off on a tangent, as it so often did nowadays, as it always had, come to think of it.

"Do you believe in ghosts?"

She blurted out the question, surprising herself. One minute she was thinking about Bess and Domino, and in the next she actually voiced the crazy notion that kept slipping into her head.

"Excuse me?"

Fenna placed her lipstick carefully down onto the dressing table and turned to face her daughter.

"Now where has all this come from?"

She was well used to Tilly's overly active imagination, and also well aware that sometimes her ideas needed to be nipped in the bud.

"Has it anything to do with that girl you keep looking for?"

Tilly lifted her chin and shrugged.

"Look, honey…"

Fenna moved across to join her on the side of the bed. "I'm not the ogre you make me out to be, you know, and if you ever need to talk then I'm here for you."

"If I can find you," grumbled Tilly.

Her mother laughed. "Well I'm here now, so why don't you tell me what's on your mind."

For Tilly it was like opening a floodgate. She went though everything, from the fire in the woods right up to her vague idea about ghosts and her thoughts on life being like a jigsaw. When she had finished talking her mother gave her a hug and for a moment they sat in silence.

"Do you know," remarked Fenna at last. "You should take up writing for a career. I don't think that I have ever met anyone with such a vivid imagination."

Tilly sat up with a relieved smile.

"So you really think it's all inside my head?"

"It is definitely all inside your head; you should listen to this Dillon friend of yours more. He makes a lot of sense. Lots of black and white horses *are* called Domino and this Bess you are always going on about probably lives on the other side of the woods. Your paths will cross eventually, believe me, and then you'll laugh at all your silly fancies. Now come on…"

She stood up and walked over to the mirror, twisting her fair hair into a knot on the top of her head.

"Forget about things that happened twenty years ago…"

"Twenty-one," murmured Tilly.

"…and get on with your life… I'll only be gone an hour or so."

Tilly let out a sigh as she watched her mother's focus slip away from her.

"OK," she agreed. "You're right. I'll have an early night and think about the future."

"Good girl," remarked Fenna absentmindedly, already reaching for her handbag.

Sleep came surprisingly easily to Tilly that night. She had expected to stay awake for hours, tossing and turning, but the moment her head hit the pillow she fell into a deep and dreamless slumber. Until something woke her just before midnight, a distant, haunting, familiar cry.

Her eyes snapped open in the darkness, struggling to focus in the velvety blackness that surrounded her. No slivers of moonlight filtered through the pale shape that was her window, no silvery stars twinkled out from the vast, impenetrable sky. All she could hear was silence, deep and powerful. So what had awakened her? She half rose, supporting herself with her elbow, and when the sound she had heard in her dreams came again, something deep inside her froze.

Night or day… She could almost hear Bess's voice in her ears. *If you ever need me…* And in that instant she knew, with no shadow of a doubt, Bess needed her now.

The cry was just a distant echo and yet, at the same time, strangely crystal clear. It seemed to come, in one moment from inside her head… and in the next… from far, far away.

"Help…! Help me. Please…"

The plea held such terror that Tilly acted without conscious thought. Bess needed her and that was enough. In seconds she was out on the landing, pulling on her jeans, sweater tucked under her arm as she raced toward the stairs. Should she call her mother? She hesitated outside Fenna's bedroom door, reaching out toward it. And in a moment that changed eternity she moved on, tiptoeing down the stairs, dragging her red sweater over her head, bursting out of the back door into the icy air of the still, dark night. Then she was running, running, running, with no conscious thought in her head other than to get to her friend.

Her feet pounded relentlessly on the pavement of the road, her breath loud and rasping, giving her rhythm and some comfort in the face of fear. All she could think of was getting to Crickle Wood with no question of why; along the narrow lane and out onto the smooth expanse of main road where not one car stirred. The moon sneaked out from behind a mass of black clouds, turning the road to a silvery ribbon where hedges and trees loomed in awesome silhouette, making her heart pound in her ears. But still she ran on, unheeding of even her own fear, on toward the deep red glow that shone from above the treetops of Crickle Wood.

As she entered the stillness of the woods smoke assailed her nostrils. Her head swam with a crackling sound that filled her ears. Fear consumed her, turning her legs into liquid that refused to do her bidding. She slowed her steps, her heart a tight, aching drum, her eyes smarting with the acrid smoke that burned her lungs.

"Help…! Help me…"

The agonizing cry brought a rush of strength that overrode all fear. Bess needed her… night or day.

"I'm coming… I'm coming… Hang on."

Unaware of the branches that cut her face she pushed through the trees, deep into the center of the woods, toward the flickering glow. Her fear was gone, pushed out by the awesome purpose that drove her. Her purpose, to save Bess.

When she burst out into the clearing she was suddenly filled by a strange sense of calm. Flames licked out from the buildings beside a single story cottage. The window glass cracked loudly with the heat, splintering onto the ground, and the doorframe was already beginning to smolder, but she knew with perfect clarity just what she had to do.

"Bess," she yelled. "Bess…!"

The cry for help cry came again, impossibly, from within the flaming furnace. Tilly raced to the open doorway, fighting against the smoke that billowed out in clouds.

"Bess…" she screamed and there she was, in the furthest

corner of the stable, heaving desperately on Domino's lead rope. The black and white cob was pressed against the back wall, head up, eyes wide with fear, nostrils flaring as red as the flames that inched toward him. Tilly plunged through the fire that was already licking at the straw beneath her feet.

Bess's eyes were rimmed with red, her face streaked with the tears that flowed freely down her cheeks. When she turned toward Tilly her face lit up with hope.

"You came…" she cried. "You heard me…"

Tilly's response was instantaneous.

"Of course I did. Now let's get you both out of here."

Above their heads a loud crack made them hesitate before redoubling their efforts.

"Please, boy," begged Bess, but the black and white gelding was way beyond reason. He stood stock still, frozen with fear despite Tilly desperately chasing him from behind while Bess heaved on the lead rope, her hands raw and bleeding.

The crack came again and Tilly glanced up to see the smoldering beam across the roof begin to bend. The roof sank, the beam burst into flame and she dragged off her jacket, tying it around Domino's head with shaking fingers.

"Get up!" she screamed, reaching for a piece of fallen plank, and with all her strength she hit him, hard across the rump. Above their heads the beam splintered, Domino leaped forward, disorientated, and she hit him again, her lungs aching with the heat and smoke. And then suddenly he was out of the door and away, knocking Bess to the ground where she lay half conscious. Tilly heaved her desperately toward the doorway, dragging her lifeless form across the ground. The beam cracked again for the final time and with one final, mighty effort, they were through the door, gulping in the nectar of sweet, fresh air while behind them the roof came crashing down.

"Domino," moaned Bess, sitting up.

"He's safe, he's safe."

Tears flooded down Tilly's cheeks as she supported her friend, and together they walked hesitantly forward where the black and white gelding stood snorting by the trees.

Tilly stirred and woke, remembering the dream, trembling with the memory and trying to force it out of her mind. Light filtered in through her window, outlining familiar things. The rosettes carefully pinned around her mirror, the huge, brown teddy bear she had been give for her very first birthday. The dream flooded back, the flames, the fear, and Bess's cries. She sat up sharply, throwing back her covers. The end of the dream was vague and shadowy. She remembered walking home in the darkness, remembered the feel of the Millennium gate, cold hard steel beneath her fingers, real and solid. But she hadn't walked home, had she? It was all just a stupid dream. Tears flooded her eyes; it had all been so terrifyingly real.

As soon as she saw her clothes, discarded on the rug beside the bed, alarm bells rang inside her head. They were streaked with dirt… and the smell. The blood pounded in her ears as she lifted them up one by one, breathing in the acrid scent of smoke. Waves of panic made her weak as she grabbed all her clothes and raced into the bathroom, hurling them into the hamper and cramming on the lid. When she looked up and caught her reflection in the mirror panic swelled inside her in an uncontrollable tide. For the image that stared out at her forced her to face the truth… A truth that would haunt her dreams forever.

Her stark white face was covered in cuts and bruises, dark marks streaked her skin and her hair hung lank and lifeless. She took a lock between shaking fingers, drawing it around to cover her face, breathing in the acrid scent of smoke with numb acceptance. It hadn't been a dream.

Warm water rushed over her head and she turned her face toward it, eyes tightly closed, washing away the telltale signs of fire and smoke. But the truth remained intact however hard she scrubbed her tender skin, and when, finally, she emerged from the shower, pink and shining with her efforts, the memories of the living dream still filled her heart and mind. She tried to sort things out inside her head as she pulled on fresh clean clothes. She had saved Bess and Domino; that was good, wasn't it? But how… and why? So many whys, vague and formless, images inside her head that surely couldn't be real.

She ran down the stairs and into the kitchen, eager for human companionship, but all that remained of her mother was a note on the kitchen table.

Hope you had a nice sleep-in, sleepy head. Couldn't bear to wake you, so those horses and chickens will have to wait for once. Where did you go yesterday? Better put your clothes in the washing machine. Have a nice day.
Love, Mom xxxxx

Tilly pedaled down the lane with shaking legs, eager to get to Cricklewood Farm and the no-nonsense, practical attitude of Dillon. He would laugh at her when she told him her story, she was sure of it. She tried to imagine his face, with its larger than life smile and twinkling eyes, but it evaded her. All she could think of was Bess and the beam that came crashing down only inches behind them. She didn't dare allow her thoughts to drift toward Elizabeth Malone. That was far too great a coincidence to even contemplate.

She didn't see the ancient four-wheel drive until it pulled alongside, engine drumming in her ears as it rattled to a standstill. The window wound down slowly, sticking half way, and when Roland Cuthbert's round face materialized behind it she pulled on her brake, stepped to the ground and gave him a friendly smile.

"Good morning…"

"I'll give you good morning, young lady, when you have paid what you owe me."

"Pardon…?"

Tilly's smile faded as confusion flooded in.

"What do you mean?"

He fought with the window, swearing under his breath, but it refused to budge.

"You know full well what I mean, young lady. You owe me a month's board and I mean to get it."

"But you said…"

She shook her head slowly.

"You were in a good mood that day. Your wife said that a relative had died and left you some money... you said it didn't matter…"

His face slowly turned beet red as he leaned across toward her.

"Have you totally taken leave of your senses, girl? The only relative I had is definitely not likely to have left me anything in his will; I didn't even go to the darned funeral. So you can forget that as an excuse…"

Behind them a car horn honked impatiently and he turned and waved his fist at it before turning back to Tilly.

"I'll get my money… you'll see," he roared, standing on the throttle. The cumbersome vehicle pulled away in a cloud of thick black smoke, leaving Tilly standing at the edge of the road with a knot in the pit of her stomach. She felt as if her whole life was turning upside down.

The gates of Cricklewood Farm stood open, familiar and

welcoming. Tilly placed her bicycle against the wall and ran across to the barn, eager to lose herself in the mundane tasks of feeding and grooming and mucking out. Sunny tossed his head in welcome and life slipped back one notch toward normality.

To her disappointment she saw someone had already laid a thick new bed of straw, and his hay net was bulging. "Dillon," she murmured affectionately. He must have done it for her when he realized she was so late. She slipped into the stable and put her arms around the big gelding's thick neck, pressing her face against the warm softness of his coat and breathing in his comforting familiar aroma while tears pricked the backs of her eyelids. Sunny pulled contentedly at his hay net as she poured out the story of her nightmare, well used to listening to his mistress's whispered ramblings and totally unaffected by her displays of emotion.

"… and I don't know if it was real or a dream," she finished, standing back. He looked at her with shining eyes, nodding his head gently, and she gave him one last hug before turning to look across to where the new horse, Jigsaw, nickered at her, eager for attention. When she rubbed her hand across his broad white face he pushed against the door, impatient to be out.

"Get back, boy," she ordered, peering over the door to make sure that he too had been fed and watered, and as he lifted his head and moved away, suddenly she noticed a freshly painted sign, just like the one that Dillon had made for Sunny.

DOMINO

The name glared out at her. What was going on… why had Dillon done that to her… was it some kind of sick joke? He knew how she felt about Bess's cob and the other Domino from all those years ago. Emotion flooded over her and all thoughts of grooming Sunny fled. The horse was called Jigsaw; Dillon had been so excited about the name…

Breathlessly she raced across the yard toward the back door, bursting through into the large sunny kitchen. Bob Atkins sat at the head of the large pine kitchen table, loaded fork poised in mid-air. He placed it carefully back down onto his plate, looking up at her reassuringly as if he was used to his breakfast being rudely interrupted.

"If you're looking for Dillon he's gone into town with his mother, but he said to tell you that he's done the horses and he'll be back later on."

"Oh…"

For a moment Tilly was speechless, her mouth moving soundlessly. He pushed back his chair and stood up, concern clouding his blue eyes.

"Are you all right, hon?"

She forced herself to smile.

"Yes… yes… of course. I just…"

Despair overwhelmed her. She had to tell someone…

"He's changed the name…"

"Name…?"

"The horse's name... Jigsaw. He was going to be called Jigsaw after…"

Needing reassurance she glanced across toward the small mahogany table upon which Dillon had so painstakingly pieced together Elizabeth's jigsaw. It was empty, apart from one magazine thrown haphazardly onto its shiny surface. The breath froze in her throat.

"It's gone…"

Bob stepped toward her, his forehead drawn into worried frown.

"Look, hon… I think you'd better sit down."

"No…!"

She forced a more composed expression onto her face, trying to get past the pounding of her heart.

"I'm fine… it's just…"

What could she tell him? Would he believe her? He looked at her with Dillon's eyes and she blundered on.

"Do you remember the girl I told you about? The girl from the woods?"

He sat back down, nodding earnestly, wanting to help.

"Oh, yes… the one who almost burned to death all those years ago."

"Almost…?"

One moment her heart was pounding in her ears and in the next it seemed to stop altogether. Seemingly unaware of her distress, Bob Atkins went back to his breakfast.

"How about a nice cup of tea?" he suggested.

Hysterical laughter bubbled in Tilly's throat. Her world was turning upside down and he was offering her a cup of tea.

She looked across toward where the completed jigsaw had been, remembering the expression on Dillon's face when he had proudly shown it to her. Was she going mad? Suddenly she knew what she had to do.

"I have to go," she mumbled, already moving toward the door. "Tell Dillon I'll be back later."

"See you," he called, shaking his head. Teenage girls! Who ever knew *what* they were thinking?

chapter eleven

It seemed to Tilly that she could see everything through a haze, like an outsider looking in. The white blur of unfamiliar faces, each intent upon their own business. Gaudy shop windows already resplendent with Christmas cheer; familiar sights that now seemed alien. Nothing could get past the images that kept on going around and around inside her head… and Bob Atkins' innocent, soul-destroying remark. "*Almost* burned to death." What had he meant by that? Her whole world seemed to be crumbling around her and she didn't know what to do.

Her fingers clutched the sides of her seat as the bus swung onto Main Street and shuddered to a halt outside Cricklewood town hall. Ahead of her eager shoppers filled the aisle, throwing her annoyed glances as she pushed past them and then she was out on the street and running… running.

She stopped outside the Gazette office, suddenly unsure. Why was she here? What did she hope to find? Instinct had drawn her, brought about by Bob Atkins' remark, but why hadn't she just stayed and talked to him instead of rushing off to find out… What… what would she find? A shudder ran through her, leaving her shivering and breathless. She was afraid of what she might find... that was the real truth.

There was a different person behind the counter, a dark-haired girl, young and helpful.

"Of course," she said, brown eyes smiling. "If you know

144

Peter Rawcliffe then I'm sure it'll be fine. He'll be down there somewhere anyway."

When Tilly ran down the stairs and entered the long, narrow storeroom she saw him at once. White head bent forward over a desk, scribbling notes on a lined pad.

He looked up with a smile.

"Ah, the girl with the school project. More information, is it?"

She nodded mutely and he moved at once toward a pile of newspapers, flicking through them until he found the right one. Tilly felt as if her heartbeat was about to take over her whole body.

"Here we are."

He was smiling at her as if it was just an ordinary day while her world came crashing down.

SAVED BY A STRANGER

A terrible tragedy was averted recently when a stranger arrived just in time to save the lives of fifteen-year-old Elizabeth Malone and her horse, Domino, from a fire that raged in his stable... stable... stable ....

The words swam before Tilly's eyes, in and out of focus as she tried to take in the awesome facts that stared out at her; Elizabeth's face – Bess's face – smiling widely, arms wrapped tightly around Domino's neck. A sob rose in her throat. She had finally gone completely mad.

"Are you all right...? Here."

Peter Rawcliffe stepped toward her, hand extended as she rose to her feet, pushing back her chair.

"Sit down," he urged but his plea fell on deaf ears. Tilly was way beyond reason, way beyond sitting down and talking about it. No one could ever understand; no one would ever believe her. She didn't even believe it herself...

"I… I have to go…"

"Wait…"

As she turned toward the stairs he followed awkwardly, calling her back. It didn't seem right to let her run off like that when she was obviously in such a state, but what could he do? What did he know about distraught young girls? As Tilly burst out into the bustling street, panic flooding her every pore, he was already going back to look at the story that had caused her such concern. "Saved by a stranger," he murmured, reading the words out loud. Now that's odd. Was that really the same story they had looked at last time? For a moment he studied the print, as if expecting it to give him some answers. The girl stared out at him, laughing gaily, and he shook his head, trying to clear it of the vague uneasiness that rankled. He felt as if there was something missing but he couldn't quite place his finger on what.

Tilly's brain felt totally numb. There was only one thing left to do now, only one way to find out the truth. She would go to the woods, to Elizabeth's cottage; surely there she would find her answer. And on the way she would call at Cricklewood Farm and get Sunny. It might give her more confidence riding there, and she desperately needed an injection of confidence from somewhere.

Secretly she hoped that Dillon might be home. Maybe he would listen to her story and understand. But how could he when she didn't understand it herself? A sob gurgled in her throat and her hands felt cold and clammy as they clutched the rail of the seat in front.

"You all right, dear?"

A round face loomed over her. Small, bright eyes, dimpled chin, kindly and caring.

For a moment she hesitated before shaking her head vigorously. What was she thinking?

146

"Yes… I'm fine, honestly." She managed a watery smile and the woman turned away to talk to her companion, unconvinced.

She felt both pairs of eyes on her back as she swayed down the aisle five minutes later. The bus rumbled to a stop at the end of her lane and as she almost fell onto the road with wobbly legs she caught a final glimpse of the woman's moon shaped face through the window above her. There was no sign now of sympathy in her bright little eyes, just pursed, disapproving lips and a slowly shaking head. Ridiculously, Tilly felt a giggle rise inside her. The giggle died and desolation flooded back as she headed up the road at a jog.

Dillon wasn't home. She knew he wouldn't be, but still disappointment clawed at her. Reaching up for Sunny's tack, she hesitated. Perhaps she should wait until he came home and then they could go together. The thought of having a companion in her search made the shivering sensation that had been with her all day retreat just a little. But what if he didn't come back until it was almost dark and what if he wouldn't listen and what if his dad gave him lots of jobs to do? No, there was only one thing to do. She had to go by herself.

The autumn sun was already sinking in the sky as she trotted out through the gates of Cricklewood Farm. Beneath her Sunny pranced, eager to be on his way and totally unaware of the turmoil going through his mistress's head. She leaned forward to press her face against the familiar warmth of his neck, allowing a few of the ever-present tears to squeeze out from behind her eyelids and soak into his silky coat. He jogged on regardless, and she found herself talking to him, telling him the whole story. It helped, she found, to say it all out loud, and by the time they reached the entrance to the woods she felt just a bit more positive.

147

The Millennium gate loomed out against the shadowy pathway beyond, solid and real. It was a barrier... but a barrier against what? She shuddered, gripping Sunny's reins so hard that her fingers ached. Every sensible bone in her body screamed at her to turn back, and for a moment she hesitated. Perhaps she should just go back to Cricklewood Farm and come again tomorrow with Dillon. The moment passed. There were too many stones left unturned, too many things that didn't add up. She had to know now, for better or worse. The gate clanged shut behind them. Sunny's hooves thudded softly on the carpet of dying leaves and she thrust out her chin, drawing on inner reserves of courage.

"I'm coming, Bess," she murmured, urging him into trot, and then they were cantering, a slow, balanced, wonderful canter that took her breath away and made everything seem real again.

When they burst through the trees into the clearing, for a moment Tilly felt as if her heart had stopped beating. The scene was so normal and yet so strange. Burnished rays of setting sun poured across the open space like liquid gold, lighting up the white picket fence that surrounded the beautifully tended cottage. A goat bleated from its tether beside the trees and golden brown chickens scratched in the earth around the garden gate. Everything was in the same place. The long, low, single story cottage that she had seen empty and derelict that day with Dillon, and again... last night... She shuddered, remembering the roar of the flames and the terrified screams that had met her then.

For a moment she wanted to turn and gallop away. It was all just too much to take in. A cold, silent wave of fear flooded her senses and her numb fingers shook as she gathered up her reins in readiness.

"Hello..."

The woman who appeared from the cottage shaded her eyes and called again.

"May I help you…?"

Tilly froze. The moment to run was gone and she prepared herself to face the truth.

The woman was in her mid-thirties or thereabouts. She was small but sturdily built, her face tanned nut brown by the summer sun, her soft brown eyes familiar and welcoming.

"Bess…?"

Tilly breathed the name that had been on her lips for so long… But how could it be?

The woman smiled.

"I knew you'd come one day," she said, reaching out for Sunny's rein. "I've been waiting for this day for twenty-one years, and so has someone else. Come with me."

Tilly slipped to the ground without conscious thought, looping Sunny's reins over her arm. She didn't allow her mind to focus on why. It was far too late for that. She just followed where Bess led, content to let events overtake her.

The stable was still there, but no signs of fire or neglect marked its solid appearance. Ivy grew up the mottled gray stone walls and the door gleamed with fresh white paint. She felt as if she were in a dream. Or was the dream from before and this was reality? Confusion left her weak and breathless.

Outside the stable, in a tiny paddock, grazed an elderly black and white cob. It raised its head from the sparse grass and peered at the new arrivals from behind its bushy forelock, nickering gently. Tilly gasped, heart racing and hand outstretched.

"Domino…?" she breathed, unable to believe that this really could be Bess's horse from so long ago… But it wasn't long ago, was it? It was just last night… Last night she had saved him from the fire. And then her arms were wrapped around his thick neck, her face pressed against his rough coat breathing in

149

his horsy aroma as if it were the most expensive perfume in the world.

Bess stood beside Sunny, holding the big dun gelding's reins in her hand and drinking in the scene before them with a calm serenity.

"I knew you'd come," she repeated.

Tilly's mind was in turmoil.

"But how?" she whispered, looking up. "How did you know?"

As the plump black and white cob wandered off, his movements stiff and slow, Tilly suddenly noticed how age had taken its toll on the once sprightly gelding. This wasn't the Domino she had saved from the fire last night. Cold fingers of panic tightened around her lungs and she looked at Bess with pleading eyes.

"How…?" she repeated.

"You saved our lives," responded Bess in a matter-of-fact tone. "That night, twenty-one years ago, you came and saved our lives. Do you remember the day when I stopped Sunny from galloping out into the road with you? You told me then that if I ever needed help you would be there for me at any time."

"Night or day," breathed Tilly.

"Night or day," echoed Bess. "And on the night of the fire I called for help and you were there. I don't know how it happened. Maybe somehow our paths crossed at an opening in time. Maybe we were both just in the right place at the right time, but somehow I believe that you came from the future to save us from the fire, and that time in the future… is now."

"But what about Elizabeth?" gasped Tilly. "And how did you know?"

Bess shrugged

"My name is Elizabeth, Elizabeth Malone, but my dad always called me Bess."

A shadow drifted across her sunny features.

151

"He died a month ago…"

The words swam around inside Tilly's head as things clicked into place. Malone… Malone… Malone. A memory of Meg Cuthbert's happy smile sprang unbidden into her mind. *A relative, Robert Malone, has died and left us some money…* And Roland Cuthbert's face that morning, so angry… It couldn't be.

"How did you know?" she repeated urgently.

"At first I didn't," admitted Bess. "Although that first time I met you I thought you looked a bit strange in those green checked jodhpurs. Afterwards I searched and searched for you. I went to Millside cottage but it was a ruin that obviously hadn't been lived in for years, and I remembered that you told me it had just been renovated. And that day in the woods, after Sunny bolted with you, you kept rambling on hysterically about the gate being gone. It was a special gate you said, put there to mark the new millennium. At the time I thought you were a bit crazy, but then, eventually, to mark the new millennium, sure enough the village decided to put a special gate into Crickle Wood. That really made me think, and I watched and waited to see if anything happened to Millside cottage. A couple of years ago they started working on it, and I've been waiting for you ever since."

Tilly tried to take in everything Bess was telling her, but it was all just too much.

"And you never told anyone?"

"Who could I tell? Who would believe me? 'Someone traveled through time to save my life.' No… I just watched and waited for you to come. I knew you would when the time was right… Here, let me show you something."

She beckoned Tilly to follow her to the front door of the cottage, handed over Sunny's rein and disappeared inside, re-emerging moments later clutching what looked like a framed picture.

"I found this in a shop not long after we first met and I had to have it because it looked so like you and Sunny. I didn't actually put it together until after the fire, though, and then I hung it on the wall to remind me of what you looked like."

Tilly felt herself recoil as Bess turned the picture to face her. She knew what it was at once but everything inside her shrank away from the awesome facts it forced her to face. That Bess really was telling the truth.

Her image stared out at her, disfigured by the tiny lines of the jigsaw pieces and her heart clamped tight shut.

Bess reached out and closed her hand around Tilly's arm, her grip real and solid.

"However scary it might feel to believe what I have told you, just remember, you saved our lives and surely that makes everything worthwhile."

Tilly felt a warm singing sensation deep inside.

"I did, didn't I?" she murmured, looking across to where Domino grazed contentedly. "And at least I have found you at last, even if you are a bit older than I expected. I can't believe that you kept such a secret for all these years."

A frown flitted across Bess's face and she glanced away.

"Well…" she began.

"Well what?" asked Tilly.

"There has always been that worry… you know."

Alarm bells rang inside Tilly's head.

"What worry?"

"The worry that something terrible will happen because we've changed the past…"

Memories flooded Tilly's mind. Roland Cuthbert's angry face, the jigsaw missing from the surface of the shiny mahogany table, the story in the paper…

Far above them the treetops whispered an unknown song and she tightened her arms around herself as a sudden, icy breeze, rippled across the clearing. Sunny pulled back, shying away from an invisible foe. Black clouds rolled angrily across the autumn sun and the afternoon sky grew suddenly as dark as night.

Trembling uncontrollably she glanced across toward the cottage. For one long, endless moment it appeared, unbelievably, to be a crumbling ruin again.

"Night or day," murmured Bess, moving closer.

"Night or day," echoed Tilly desperately… as she turned to meet the nut-brown gaze of the fifteen-year-old girl who stood staunchly beside her.

For an instant she saw flames once again, crackling hungrily. A hollow scream echoed around inside her head and her fingers reached for Bess's arm. The past and the present were fused into one timeless zone, yesterday today and tomorrow, a single blurry image with no boundaries to hold them.

And then she heard a voice, solid and real in the face of confusion… Dillon's voice. The present clicked firmly back into alignment.

"I thought I'd find you here," he said, slipping down from his horse's broad back and casually looping the reins over his arm. "Now don't you think it's time you told me what is going on?"

"You'd never believe it," she murmured.

"Try me," he insisted, walking purposefully toward her.

For a moment she glanced across toward the Bess she had finally met today, nut brown and solid and very, very real.

"This is my friend Bess," she announced proudly.

Dillon held out his hand, and as the fingers of both her friends firmly interlocked suddenly everything clicked into place. The past was behind them and whatever it was that had happened there it no longer mattered. For this was their future, right here and now.

"Glad to meet you at last," he said. "I was beginning to think that Tilly had made you up."

154